Two

CIA MULES

Two
CIA MULES

Seth Moorhead

Another Quality Book Published By:

LEGACY BOOK PUBLISHING

1883 Lee Road, Winter Park, FL 32789

www.LEGACYBOOKPUBLISHING.com

Two CIA Mules

Published by:
LEGACY Book Publishing
1883 Lee Road
Winter Park, Florida 32789
www.LegacyBookPublishing.com

©2022 Seth Moorhead
Printed in the United States
ISBN: 978-1-958923-26-9

Cover Design by Gabriel H. Vaughn

Dedication

This book is dedicated to my daughter, Jennifer, whose enthusiastic editing was invaluable.

 **A NOTE FROM THE AUTHOR**

This book contains two stories; a comedy about how two mules were used by the CIA to prevent suicide bombing and how they also were the catalysts for several love stories.

Although the book is entirely a work of fiction, it contains some people and events that are true. This novel's story and characters are fictitious. Certain long-standing institutions, agencies, and public offices are mentioned, but the characters involved are wholly imaginary. The author, Seth Moorhead, is ever grateful to the CIA for being invited to give a lecture there on U.S. Navy equipment while employed by Martin Marietta (now Lockheed Martin) and is highly respectful of them.

TABLE OF CONTENTS

 # CHARACTERS

Susan O'Connor— FBI agent, liaison with the CIA
Hugh Montague— CIA agent, working directly for the President of the United States
Tom Jacobs— CIA Director of Animals Department
Jane Dogan— Friend of Kate living in North Carolina
Kate Smithfield— Friend of Jane living in Florida
Henry Dogan— Jane's husband
Jim Smithfield— Kate's husband
Ruth Cohen— Architect, daughter of Jacob Cohen
Jacob Cohen— French Architect, student of Frank Lloyd Wright
Eve Cohen— Adopted daughter of Jacob Cohen
Francois Allard— Adopted brother of Boss
Henri Blanchet— Adopted brother of Boss
Boss— Muslim leader seeking to avenge father's death
Ward— Mule ridden by Jane (depicted above)
Heather— Mule ridden by Kate (depicted above)
John Smith— Owner of mules
President— The President of the United States
Betty O'Connor— Susan's Mother
Camille— Lady from France
Andrew, Barbara, and Charlie— Hugh's children

 **CHAPTER ONE**

The President's Assignment

Susan nervously stood in front of the mirror and said, "First impressions are important." Her boss at the FBI had given her a new assignment, and she was to meet Hugh Montague of the CIA today. She grabbed different suits and business dresses from the closet and held each up as she considered them in the mirror. What would make a good impression on Mr. Montague? As she pondered her dilemma, she thought of how her dad would be proud of her for this promotion to the position of liaison with the CIA and felt a tinge of sorrow at what she missed sharing with him since his passing. Shaking herself back to the present, she knew that her mom would, at any rate, be duly impressed once she wrote to tell her about it.

Yesterday, her boss called her in and said, "I've found a new assignment for you that I think you will be uniquely qualified for. Now that you have been with us for almost five years, it's time for you to get out of the office and learn as much as you can about the CIA. You will be their FBI coordinator for operations within the U.S.A. for whatever assignment the President has given Hugh Montague there. He will be expecting you in his office at 9 a.m. Monday morning."

Finally, deciding the light blue print dress with the accompanying navy-blue jacket was sufficiently business enough, she dressed, pushed some mousse through her short blonde curly hair, applied some basic make-up, and checked her look one more time. Satisfied she was sufficiently presentable, she grabbed her coffee and briefcase and headed out.

Susan glanced at the beautiful, blue-sky day and decided to put the top down on her little red VW Bug for her drive to work. She made a note to thank her mom again for leaving her such a great place to live where she could drive up the George Washington Memorial Parkway each morning on the way to work at the FBI office in Washington, D.C. With the canopy formed over the highway by the huge trees on both sides of the road, it's such a beautiful drive almost any time of the year. There is such a variety of trees in the area that in the fall, there is a riot of bright colors; red, orange, and golden leaves everywhere, while the spring boasts a variety of dark and light green leaves as new buds appear. Now it was May, and the Cherry Blossoms were in full bloom all along the parkway. This time, however, she wouldn't be driving to her office but to the offices of the CIA.

It is a longer but more pleasant drive because she stays on the George Washington Memorial Parkway past all the turnoffs to Washington, D. C., until she reaches the proper turnoff in McLean, Virginia.

While driving along the parkway, Susan reviewed the things her FBI supervisor had told her yesterday. He said that it was a highly classified mission and that he did not know the details because he did not have the "need to know." The only thing that he did know was that the President of the United States had given an assignment directly to a man named Hugh Montague in the CIA and that he would need the assistance of the FBI to carry it out. He said further that he had been told to send the best person he could spare for the job and that he felt sure it would offer her a good opportunity for advancement.

The CIA headquarters was surrounded by parkland and government-owned land. Susan's first glimpse of the building was somewhat intimidating. It was massive. *So*, she thought, *this is what 1.4 million square feet of office space looks like.* As she pulled up to the gate, a security guard greeted her. "Good morning, Susan," he said. She was surprised.

"How come you know my name, but I don't know yours?"

"That's alright. We have been expecting you. My name is John. Just pull up over there and leave the keys in the car so I can move it if I have to."

As she pulled over and parked, a blue Ford Hybrid did the same beside her, and she noticed a tall, handsome young man in a brown suit get out. From reviewing his dossier, Susan knew it was Hugh Montague. Hugh was 30 years old, a little over six feet tall, and had thick dark hair and brown eyes. She cracked a smile when she noticed that his brown suit was so wrinkled it looked like he had slept in it the night before. Typical. Geniuses rarely consider their appearances, and Hugh was a genius. It only took him three years to graduate from Johns Hopkins University with a Master's degree in mathematics. After graduating, he worked for Martin Marietta in Orlando, Florida, as an Advanced Design Engineer where, among other things, he helped write proposals for new business.

Susan heard that Hugh had a unique capability to solve problems other people wouldn't even try. A simple illustration occurred one day on a trip to Washington, D. C. to visit a potential customer. He was expected to meet with others at 7:30 a.m. for breakfast. When he showed up a few minutes late, his reason was, "I woke up and realized I needed a haircut more than I needed breakfast." How could he find a barber shop open that early in the morning? When asked, he didn't.

He had gone to a dog groomer and convinced her he needed help and would pay her well if she would cut his hair. Only Hugh would have the confidence and nerve to get a dog groomer to give him a good haircut.

"Hello Hugh, I'm Susan O'Connor." She decided that he must be single because no wife would let him go to work so rumpled-looking. So much for first impressions.

"Hello!" Hugh replied, "You must be the new member of my team." As Susan walked toward him, he couldn't help but be drawn to her bright blue eyes, ready smile, and how the curls of her blonde hair bounced around the soft features of her face. *Cute as a button,* he thought to himself, *I expect she is also smart as a whip. Otherwise, the FBI wouldn't have selected her to coordinate with us.*

"It's good to have such a pretty girl as our FBI coordinator. Come with me, and I will show you to my office, which will be our office for a while." Susan smiled and wondered just how long it would take him to realize that she was more than just a "pretty girl."

As they walked up to the building, Susan stopped beside the courtyard and stared questioningly at the tall scroll sculpture made of copper. She looked at Hugh, "What an odd sculpture. Does it have some special meaning?" she asked.

Hugh stopped with her and looked at the sculpture he seldom noticed or thought about.

"Well," he said, "it is obviously the Kryptos. See the thousands of punched through letters? It is rumored that it holds an encrypted message that is yet to be cracked."

Susan looked closer at the letters Hugh had pointed out. "How long has it been there?" she asked.

"I don't know," Hugh responded. "Probably 30 years or so."

As they walked on, Susan tried to make small talk. "This building has not been here very long, has it? I heard that the cornerstone was laid by President Eisenhower in 1959."

Hugh continued to walk on, not looking at her but at least willing to converse.

"That's right. The building was not completed until 1963, and in 1990, it was officially renamed the George H. W. Bush Center for Intelligence."

Pausing, he opened the door to his office and walked in ahead of her.

Once in his office, Hugh continued straight to the chair behind his desk. Susan only took one step into the room and stood stock-still looking around to take it all in. She thought, *I've seen a lot of offices but none like this.*

It is a corner office with all windows on two sides. As Hugh sat and began to look through papers on his desk, Susan noticed the beautiful view of the landscape and the Potomac River. The rest of the office was furnished like a comfortable living room.

Along one wall was a large comfortable sofa with end tables and table lamps, while the other wall contained two over-stuffed chairs, each with an ottoman and a table with a lamp of its own. The striking thing was that each of the four tables contained a clock and what looked like an old-fashioned telephone. Three of the clocks all showed different times, while the phones alongside them contained two small lights, a green and a red one. Two of the phones had their green lights on. The fourth phone, next to one of the chairs, had its clock set at noon and turned off.

In front of the sofa was a coffee table, while in the corner was a cabinet containing supplies and a coffee maker.

After taking it all in, Susan said, "Wow, what an office. I've never seen anything like this!"

Smiling, Hugh replied, "Thank you. It does have all the conveniences of home."

"I assume those clocks are showing the local time at several places around the world, but what do the red and green lights mean?"

Hugh points to each clock in turn, saying, "That's London, that's Paris, and that's Tokyo. When the green light is on, it means someone is near the phone and is available to take my call. When the red light is on, it means they are calling me. The fourth one, which is not in use, is ready to be set up wherever we need it."

Nodding, Susan said, "So, you can really communicate instantly anywhere; and I am sure they are all hooked up to coded scramblers. That's impressive."

"Yes," Hugh replied, "This was a trail blazed by Winston Churchill and Franklin Roosevelt during World War II. Even Churchill's staff thought that little room Churchill went to occasionally was a washroom. After the war was over, they discovered it only contained a telephone with a direct line to Roosevelt."

As Hugh talked to her, he couldn't help but again take in how beautiful she was. Her blue eyes were disarmingly gorgeous, and her short, cropped blonde hair softly framed her lovely face. He suddenly felt a little awkward as he remembered his manners, admonishing himself for not holding the door open to let her walk in first and failing to offer her a cup of coffee. Quickly, to correct this, he got up from his desk and walked across to the coffee machine, saying, "I'll fix us some coffee; then we must get acquainted while I explain our problem. Take a seat anywhere you like."

Susan glanced around and quickly sat down near the center of the couch where she could conveniently reach the coffee table, hoping he would sit down beside her.

Again admonishing himself for not asking how she took her coffee, Hugh ran his hand through his dark hair and turned to her.

"Cream, sugar, or both?" he asked.

"I like my coffee blonde but not sweet, thank you." She replied.

Once he had made himself his usual backup cup and poured sufficient cream into hers, he turned and brought the coffees over, handing Susan hers before taking a seat beside her on the couch. Taking a few quick sips of his steaming coffee to get himself back into work mode, Hugh began to explain:

"The President wants us to make sure there are no suicide bombings by terrorists in this country and to do it in such a way to achieve good publicity. It will be a very tricky thing to do, requiring some careful planning. Since the CIA is not allowed to operate within the United States, all our local work will be handled by you."

"I can't believe you haven't found a way to work around that requirement," Susan said, raising her eyebrows and blowing on her coffee before taking a sip.

"Well, we have, partly, but only within certain limits. We use something we call 'Deep Cover.'"

"That sounds interesting," she says, suddenly becoming even more attentive. "Tell me about it."

"Deep Cover is a method of transmitting messages using people who do not know they are doing it for the CIA. For instance, a person with a seeing-eye dog. With the arrangements made ahead of time by two of our agents, one could put a message on the dog another could take it off without the owner knowing that it was there. It's not fool-proof, but it works more often than not."

"But what happens if the person finds out?"

"That's where the FBI comes in. We only use people that have been cleared earlier as prospective FBI hires so that if that happens, we either stop using them or get you to hire them either temporarily or permanently."

"So, I guess that means you have to have access to our personal files?"

"Yes, but only the inactive files, the ones where you decided not to hire the person for some reason."

"Why would we even have such files?"

"For future uses in cases they have shown some particular ability or talent that someone like the CIA would find useful. You probably never realized it, but when you were in college, the FBI had spotted you as a potential agent and had you under surveillance before making you an offer."

"No kidding! I had no idea. I guess it's pretty harmless, but it seems kind of sneaky to me."

"It confirms their efficiency," Hugh said, praising the FBI, which was unusual for him.

"That's amazing! Maybe I can find my own file someday and see what it says. But that's enough about me. Let's get back to the problem."

"Right. We heard, from various sources, that there is a radical group among the Muslim teachers in Algiers, so we bugged some of their classrooms and discovered a meeting they were having. However, they found and destroyed all but one of the listening devices, and all we heard after that was a lot of writing on the blackboard. They are trying to recruit and train suicide bombers, but that's all we know."

"How about names. Did we get any names?"

Hugh smiled as he appreciated her use of the word "we." It assured him that she was on his team and ready to work.

"No, they didn't use names except to call one of them the Boss," he replied.

"I assume they moved their meeting place as soon as they found those bugs. Do we know anything about that?" Susan asked as her thoughts began to work on the problem.

"No, but if they are smart, they will move it outdoors to maintain secrecy. The only thing we are doing about it now is watching for anyone who might leave Algiers and come to the United States. There is one pair of tourists, Francois Allard and Henri Blanchet, who have made plane reservations next week and appear to be on their way from Algiers to Las Vegas via Paris and New York. Still, there is nothing suspicious about them, except that they are English language teachers."

"I wouldn't think they would need any English language teachers. If you are training suicide bombers, you could find plenty of Muslims who speak English in both France and England," Susan said as she sipped her still too hot coffee.

"Well, it's not much of a lead, but I think, Susan, you might alert your FBI office in Las Vegas to keep an eye on them for us."

"Sure, I can do that. What else can you suggest, Hugh?" Susan asked.

She felt like he was sending her down a rabbit hole with his first request.

"I would like to spend some more effort trying to eavesdrop on the meeting in Algiers. If I were trying to have a secret meeting, I would have it outdoors at some remote location that could only be reached by walking or riding a horse to assure there was no possible way to be bugged."

"Sounds like you have some pondering to do," Susan said.

She looked around the room again and realized that although the office was certainly spacious, there was no adequate space for both of them to work in the same spot.

Using her best Southern charm, she turned to Hugh and said, "I would like to go ahead and make some phone calls to see what I can do about having an agent at the airport when your suspects arrive and tail them for a few days, but I don't want to disturb you and all the important business you have to attend to. Do you think it would be possible, in this vast building, that perhaps there is a small office nearby? All I need is a chair, desk, phone, and some privacy? A girl needs some space she can call her own," she teased, batting her eyes at him.

"Of course, I should have thought of that," Hugh stammered as he walked over to a phone to call down to administration.

"Hello, this is Hugh Montague. There is a small office two doors down from me that I need for our FBI liaison, Susan O'Connor. Please make sure the phone in that room is turned on and bring some office supplies up: pens, notepads, laptop."

"I have my laptop with me," Susan interrupted. "I just need the wireless connection code to the internet."

Hugh repeated what she had said over the phone to the administrative officer and walked her down to the office. It also had a beautiful view through one large wall-to-wall window but was sparsely equipped with only an office chair behind a walnut desk with a phone on top. A coat rack was in the corner, and two low-backed chairs were situated in front of the desk.

"This will be fine," Susan said. "Thank you."

Hugh pointed out where the ladies' facilities were on their floor and, as he left, told her to feel free to come to his office for coffee, as his was much better than what they had to offer in the vending machines downstairs.

Within five minutes, an office worker knocked on her door with some supplies and picked up the phone to punch in a few numbers.

"You are all set, ma'am," he said. "I am supposed to remind you that phones are all on recorded lines. Here is an official extension directory. For outside calls, dial nine first."

Susan settled in, using her cell phone to call her boss to let him know how things were going. She asked about what channels she needed to go through to get the personnel assignments that Hugh needed. Once Susan received that information, she used the CIA phone to make the calls. Then she turned to her laptop to make some report notes concerning the issues and the personnel contacted. When she had finished, she turned her chair around to ponder the view, and her thoughts immediately wandered to Hugh.

He was a handsome man in a disheveled sort of way. She smiled as she thought of how he always ran his hand through his dark hair when correcting himself about something. She would love to run her hand through his hair someday. Lost in her daydream, she was startled when, without a knock, the door swung open.

"Let's go to lunch. There's a nice place in Old Town, Alexandria, called Landini's. Tom Jacobs will probably be there, and I'll get him to join us and see what he thinks."

"Who is Tom Jacobs?" Susan asked as she quickly picked up her purse and followed him out the door.

"He is our expert with animals, and I have a hunch we will need him on our team," Hugh explained.

As they walked out, Susan again felt the need to break the silence. "Let me ask you something; since the CIA does all its work in foreign countries, why do you have such a large building here?"

"Because we have a lot of people here studying and analyzing the weapon systems of other nations. It's quite a relief to them when they get to see what the United States has."

"I suppose that is a nice diversion for them."

"It is. When our navy developed a new missile launching system that overcame many of the drawbacks of the previous system, I met one of the engineers that designed a large part of it for the company now called Lockheed Martin. I invited him to come here and give a presentation of the design to our people, who were quite appreciative. They were delighted to see what a great system it was. It is always a morale booster for them to see what we have compared to our potential enemy."

 # CHAPTER TWO

Lunch at Landini's

They got into Hugh's car and headed for Landini's. It is in downtown Alexandria. As they rode down George Washington Memorial Parkway, Susan relaxed and again enjoyed the beautiful scenery alongside the Potomac River. Hugh is not much for small talk, *probably typical of a genius I.Q.,* she thought.

Again, she noticed him take his hand and run it through his hair, so she attempted to engage him in conversation.

"How do you like driving a hybrid? I was thinking about getting one, but I am enjoying my convertible too much."

Hugh took a deep breath, glad she had asked him anything, as he felt uncomfortable in the silence.

"I love it. The best part about it is how quiet it is. When you start it, there is no noise. One guy I talked to said he tried to rent one and gave up when he couldn't get it started, and he failed to realize it was already running, silently, on the battery."

He smiled as they both laughed, and Susan again thought how handsome his face looked when he relaxed and smiled.

Soon, they arrived at Landini's and pulled into a parking spot along the street. Landini's is a sea-food restaurant nestled among 3-story brick and stone buildings in the older part of town. It has minimal curbside seating, already occupied by what appeared to be tourists, so they walked inside, where there were mostly men talking quietly, apparently engaged in serious conversation.

Susan noticed a table with several FBI agents she knew and nodded to them in recognition as they walked in.

The waiter greeted Hugh like he was a regular and showed them to a table, asking them what they would like to drink. "A Beefeater's martini on the rocks for me. How about you, Susan? Relax, I'm buying."

"No, we should split the bill. A white wine for me, please," Susan said, rather curtly. She was a little nervous because she had the feeling those FBI agents were talking about her.

"Would you prefer—"

"Whatever's handy. I'm not particular."

Recognizing this as the perfect opportunity to get acquainted, Hugh said, "So, let's hear your story, Susan. How did you manage to get involved with the FBI?"

"I'm not really sure, but I'll bet my dad had something to do with it. He was in the Marines, and we traveled a lot until he finally retired in Charleston, South Carolina, where he went to work for the FBI in the ATF Division. That's Alcohol, Tax and Firearms if you are not familiar with the terminology. He was a stickler for doing things right. When he reported two of his co-workers for turning in erroneous trip reports, his boss decided he would be happier working in a different office and transferred him to Virginia. So, we moved to Virginia in time for me to go to school here."

"Is your dad still with the FBI?"

"No, he has passed away, and my mother moved back to Charleston, leaving me with a nice condo just south of Alexandria, very convenient to D. C."

Just then, the drinks arrived, and Hugh spotted Tom. "Hey Tom, come over here and join us."

Tom had a Scandinavian look to him. Tall, thin, blonde hair and green eyes. He looked old enough to be Susan's father. When he walked toward their table, Susan greeted him. As he took a seat, before he could acknowledge her, Hugh said, "This is Susan, our liaison from the FBI. Have you heard about my new assignment?"

"Hello, Susan. I'm glad to meet you," said Tom pleasantly.

Then, glancing at Hugh, he said, "Yes, I heard you were working directly for the President. That must be some important assignment. If you need some help, I'll be glad to join you."

Hugh caught Tom up on what he and Susan discussed earlier in his office and then asked, "If you were in Algiers and had to recruit suicide bombers to come here, how would you go about it?"

Before he could answer, the waiter approached to take their order. Susan went first, ordering the soft-shell crab, Hugh ordered fried oysters, and Tom decided on fried shrimp.

"Well, first, I would have my secret meetings out-of-doors, in a remote location, and change the location frequently. Then I would recruit some relatively young people that could easily get into the U.S.A. from either Paris, London, or Madrid. Then, I would look for those who already spoke English so I wouldn't have to teach them," suggested Tom.

"My thinking, exactly, Tom. But can you think of any way we can eavesdrop on their conversation while they are out-in-the-open?"

"That would be tough. If they rode horses to their meetings, maybe we could find a way to bug a horse. I know that would be very hard to do because I have tried it before, but I guess I could try it again," Tom said reluctantly.

Hugh sat back, thought for what seemed like only a few seconds, and said, "Assuming they do ride horses to their meetings, I know just how we can implement our Deep Cover message system, but we would need to find a couple of people who like to ride horses. Maybe you would like to help Susan dig through those old FBI prospective personnel files they have been saving for us."

Just then, the waiter walked up to check on drinks, but Tom didn't skip a beat, assenting to Hugh's suggestion and saying, "How about it, Susan?"

Susan, naturally cautious, stared at Tom with her mouth open. As soon as the waiter walked away, she whispered, "How can you talk about all that here? Isn't it classified?"

Hugh smiled, glad to see she was prone to be discrete in unfamiliar surroundings. Running his hand through his hair, he realized he should have reassured her. "Oh, Susan, I am sorry. I should have explained before we got here. Landini is a retired CIA agent. When he bought this place, he rebuilt it to make it secure. He wanted a nice restaurant for his CIA friends to enjoy. You'll see lots of CIA and FBI agents here."

Susan sat back and relaxed for the first time since they had come in the front door.

"Yes," she said, "I've already seen a few I know."

Just as she said that one of the FBI agents got up and came over to Susan.

He leaned over her and whispered loudly, "We've caught one. You need to come with us to help interrogate him."

Susan, eyes suddenly intent on her fellow FBI agent, gave him an assenting nod and then turned to Hugh, "Sorry, I have to leave. We've captured a terrorist. They need me because of my knowledge of The Koran."

Hugh didn't hesitate, "Go, go. Keep in touch."

Susan quickly departed with the other three FBI agents looking back and waving to Hugh.

Hugh's jaw dropped, and he stared, dumbfounded, at Tom.

Tom, just as surprised, says, "That's some girl you've got there! She's a lot more than an FBI liaison person. I would be willing to bet that she is a member of Mensa, just like you."

"I think you're right," Hugh replied as he nodded and continued his lunch.

Later that night, Susan finally arrived back at the CIA office so she could pick up her car. She noticed that Hugh's car was still there. "I wonder if he waited for me all this time. I had better go in and check," she mumbled to herself. Finding Hugh in his office, she flung open the door, excited and proud to be bringing Hugh information.

"Have I got a lot of news for you! It was a terrorist trying to bring down an airline by using a bomb in his shoe, but it didn't go off. He even tried to light it with a match before they captured him."

Hugh didn't seem surprised. He sat back with a knowing smile while Susan's eyebrows leaped up, astonished by his casual response.

He handed her a white plastic box from the restaurant, saying, "You have probably already eaten, but here's your soft-shell crab. Did he come from London?"

"That was very thoughtful of you, thanks. And he did come from London. How would you know that?"

"The problem with the bomb. That's the work of Charlie, our agent in London. He's an explosives expert, and the terrorists there think he is wonderful.

If they only knew how wonderful. There was never any danger."

Changing the subject to learn more about her, Hugh said, "I didn't know you were an FBI interrogator. They told me you were in the coordination section."

"They just want me to help because I'm the only Christian they know who is familiar with the Koran."

Hugh's eyebrows lifted in curiosity, "I'm amazed. How many languages do you know?"

"Just English and some Farsi. I read an English translation, which you need to do if you want to know anything about Muslims."

She pulled a book out of her purse and thumbed through it, looking for a specific page.

"You read to him from the Koran?" Hugh asks, amazed. He thinks the book she is handling is in Arabic.

"Yes, here it is right here. Book 4, paragraph 26, 'Do not kill yourselves. God is merciful to you, but anyone who does that through wickedness and injustice shall be burned in fire.'"

Hugh frowned. Looking serious, he said, "Stop right there. Ring your boss on your phone. I need to talk to him."

Susan was aghast. She was so nervous she could hardly handle the phone. Had she done something wrong? Had she insulted him in some way? Gritting her teeth, she calls her boss and hands Hugh the phone.

"Hello, this is Hugh Montague. I just want to thank you for sending Susan to us. I didn't realize you had people as smart as her in the FBI. And pretty too. Thanks very much," he hung up.

Susan let out a sigh of relief, suddenly so happy she was grinning from ear to ear. "You frightened me. I thought you were going to ask him to replace me."

"Not on your life!" said Hugh, smiling. "You are just the kind of person I have been looking for because you would fit right in with my plan for a College of Religions."

"What plan?"

"I'll tell you about it later. What information did you get from him?"

"He said there were five instructors that recruited him and worked with him for two months. He said they insisted he continues in his job but spent all his spare time with them. They spoke great English, but they also spoke several other languages as well. The only one he knew well enough to identify was French."

"Did you get any names?"

"No. He said that they didn't use any names. Once in a while, he said they would use the term 'Boss,' but he didn't know if that was a name or not."

As they walked out to their cars together, Hugh was reluctant to say good night. Susan felt the closeness developing between them and hoped Hugh felt it too. They quietly said good night, and each headed toward their respective cars.

 **CHAPTER THREE**

First Date

Mornings always started early for Susan and this May morning was no different. Her ritual was a two-mile run as the sun was coming up. She loved the smell and feel of the freshness of a new day as the sun gently woke the earth. Wild morning glories opened to the sun, and birds began to sing. Yes, sunrises were her favorite time. The sound of her breath in rhythm with her foot-falls moved her into a meditative state where she often allowed her mind to speak to her dad. She missed him.

They had both been early risers, and she always enjoyed their conversations in the mornings when it was just the two of them having breakfast. Sometimes, during her run, she felt he was really with her, and she would let her mind have a conversation with him as she ran.

After showering and dressing in a comfortable pantsuit, she headed back to the CIA.

She would stop by Hugh's office to say good morning, get a cup of coffee and, if he was available for a quick meeting, catch him up on what she had learned last night. She knocked on his door, opened it a crack to make sure she wasn't disturbing anything, walked in, and headed toward the coffee machine.

Hugh asked before she could sit down, "By the way, what's the latest from Las Vegas?"

"Our two guys had dinner with two young ladies from France, Ruth and Eve, and rented a car the next day to drive out to visit the Grand Canyon. They're acting like tourists except for avoiding the casinos, which seems a little strange."

"They might be avoiding casinos to keep from being photographed. Tell your agent we are interested in them, and we need to know what they are doing there."

"He assumed that. He has been watching pretty closely."

The rest of the day hummed along with various tasks on other projects. Around 5:00, Hugh, feeling uncharacteristically unsure of himself, walked over to Susan's little office and waited for her to end her phone call. "I was wondering if you would join me for dinner tonight?" he asked. "I was thinking of relaxing at a nice little place on the river that serves great steaks and usually has a nice band entertaining the locals."

"That would be nice. Do I have time to go home and change, or did you want to leave from here?"

"How about if I pick you up around 6:30? Would that give you enough time?"

"Sounds perfect. I'll head home now."

Susan smiled to herself and sang with the radio the whole way home. She quickly showered, reapplied her makeup, and found a casual sundress that showed off her curves subtly.

"You clean up real nice," Hugh said as he admired her transformation from business to casual.

Susan smiled as she again noticed that he ran his hand through his thick dark hair.

"Thank you. You don't look so bad yourself, kind sir," she said, sweetly and found herself blushing a little.

He certainly did look handsome in his jeans, white polo shirt, and dockers. He opened the car door for her, and again she smiled and thanked him. As he shut her door and headed around to his side of the car, he smiled and felt more confident in her company.

On their ride to the restaurant, Susan asked, "Tell me about your plan for a College of Religions?"

Impressed that she remembered his mention of this, Hugh was eager to talk about it.

"Alright, let me start by saying if you are going to improve the world, you have two things to choose from; education or invention. To my thinking, civilization moves forward, walking on the two legs of education and invention. Gradually, people become more educated and from time to time some brilliant person invents something great. Since I am not an inventor, I will have to do something in the way of education to make my contribution."

As Hugh warmed up to his subject, he became more intense.

"I firmly believe that the main cause of religious wars is simply the complete ignorance of people about other people's religion. If they were educated about what people of other religions truly believed, they would be much more inclined to be tolerant of them rather than trying to kill them. Your reading of the Koran is a perfect example of what I'm talking about. You might qualify as one of my first instructors."

Susan started to feel a warm glow. She felt like Hugh was beginning to think of her as a companion.

"You may have something there. The first time I read the Koran, the thing that impressed me the most was the fact that Moses, who is so prominent in both the Jewish and Christian religions, is cited over 50 times. But getting someone to study a different religion than their own would be a tremendous undertaking."

"That's true. That will be a major stumbling block. However, it's one of my favorite dreams to improve the world. I firmly believe in the value of education. You know, of course, from reading the Bible that one of the greatest things Jesus ever did was to persuade the Jewish disciples to go out into the world and teach Gentiles and everyone else about who he was. If they hadn't done it, where would we be? And, worse than that, we never thanked them. Maybe we should each find a Jewish person and thank him for what a small group of his ancestors did for us."

The early evening stop-and-go traffic started to irritate Hugh, when, with a sigh of relief, he said, "We are here," as he pulled up to valet parking, which seemed out of place for this small restaurant. The place was packed, but he had reserved a table close to the small band so they could enjoy the music while they ate. Hugh ordered a nice bottle of wine to go with their meal, and they laughed and talked about everything except work. Susan learned that he was a musician, and when she mocked disbelief, Hugh got up and asked the band leader if he could join them on their next number.

"Of course, what instrument would you like to play?" he asked.

"Any that's convenient," Hugh replied.

"Okay, can you handle that 12-string guitar over there?"

Hugh walked over, picked up the guitar, checked it to see if it was in tune, and said, "Whenever you are ready, buddy."

He played two songs using the guitar and then said his fingers needed rest. Hugh asked if he could play the harmonica on the next tune.

They indulged him because he had done so well on the guitar.

Susan sat amazed.

When the band said their next number was a blues song, Hugh asked if he could play the saxophone with them, and they again accommodated him. He did a stellar job, and Susan clapped wildly when the song finished, and the band took a break.

On the way home, Susan felt the effects of the wine and was all a-chatter about how astonished she was with Hugh's ability with the various instruments he had played. He told her she would be impressed with a friend of his who could play by ear on the piano any song she knew while using only the black keys, and she just shook her head.

As he pulled up to her condo, she turned to him and said, "Thank you for such a nice dinner, Hugh. I will see you at the office on Monday. Have a nice weekend." And she got out of the car without giving him a chance to walk her to the door.

He watched her until she went inside and pulled away, thinking this lady was worth a great deal more effort to get to know.

CHAPTER FOUR

Jane and Kate Discovered

Early the next morning Susan found herself thinking about dinner last night on the way to Hugh's office. She wondered if he was just as nervous as she was. Hugh, on the other hand, prepared Susan a cup of coffee, just how she likes it, and waited for her to arrive.

When they were finally in the room together, Susan's nerves subsided and they began discussing the information they had received from the FBI agent in Las Vegas. He had followed Francois and Henri out to the Grand Canyon and interviewed the various people they talked to there.

The agent had learned and reported that they tried to buy several mules but were turned down. They agreed to lease two of them to be shipped to Algeria to a stable there that rents out horses. It appears that they won't be sent for at least two weeks.

"Apparently, you and Tom are right, Hugh. They must be planning outdoor meetings in some, or more, remote places," Susan commented, as she took another sip of coffee.

"Yes, that is just what we expected. This could work out perfectly. We have two weeks to get our Deep Cover system set up. Susan, you and Tom need to search the old, unused personnel files and find some people that are familiar with horses or mules."

Susan checked Tom's office to see if he was available to go. They rode together in Tom's car back down the George Washington Memorial Parkway, crossing the river into the District of Columbia over to the FBI offices. The place that kept the old files on those considered for employment was a large 20 by 40-foot room jammed with nothing but filing cabinets.

"It's dusty in here," remarked Susan. "These files must not be used much."

"You are probably right," agreed Tom. "Let's start with the latest ones and work our way backward." He walked down the rows looking at dates until he found what he was looking for.

He pulled open a drawer and took out an armful of files, followed by Susan, who grabbed the next group and said, "Follow me; I'll show you an empty office just down the hall, which will be very convenient for this chore."

They sat down across from each other and went to work looking through the files for people who have some familiarity with horses.

It didn't take long for this task to get tedious, and as Susan closed her twentieth file, she asked, "Tom, how did you get so interested in various animals?"

"It's a long story," Tom replied, closing the file he had been reviewing. "I started in school learning to follow in my father's footsteps and becoming a veterinarian. Then I met a lady whose grandchild was raising ducks. She sold the eggs together with a little pamphlet on making various egg dishes. She was doing quite well with it and having a great time when some animal broke into the duck's cage, killing one and injuring the other. She told me they took the duck to an exotic animal veterinarian, and $650 later, all they had for their trouble was another dead duck. I remarked that it seemed like an awful lot of money to be charged, and she told me that's the minimum amount just to walk in the door. In fact, that's what he charged for her sick gecko."

Susan gave him a questioning look, wondering if this was a joke.

"It's true," Tom said. "I said, 'You have a pet gecko? What was the matter with him?' and she said that he was constipated."

Susan had been grinning all this time, and she finally started to laugh, "How in the world do you find out a gecko is constipated?"

Tom replied, "That's exactly what I asked. She said, 'You x-ray him, of course.'"

Susan laughed out loud, "That's a great story," she said. "You could probably write a book of all your experiences."

Tom grinned. "Anyway, that's when I decided to become an exotic animal veterinarian. My father was pleased about it, and when I graduated, we went on many trips together, visiting his vet friends all over Europe. We always had a lot to talk about. One day, we ran into a friend of my dad's in Europe who turned out to be a recruiter with the CIA. He had all kinds of theories about using animals for various purposes, and I was just the guy he was looking for. So, I joined up and wound up running the Animal Department here in Washington."

After they got nowhere with the first set of files, they returned and got another armload.

"You would think, among all these people, someone would own horses."

"They probably do, but it was never included because nothing was significant about it."

"Is there any chance we have encountered a hopeless task?"

"Maybe, but there are only a few more years to dig into."

They were back again, each with an armload of files, and after about another hour of searching, Susan suggested they take a break and go to lunch.

They walked out of the FBI building and on to D street, looking for a quiet restaurant. They found a cozy booth, and after ordering, Susan asked Tom why he seemed to be more interested in finding an association with mules rather than horses.

Tom replied that, in the past, he had tried to install listening devices on a horse or mule and thought it would be easier in the mule's ear because it was larger. But even though the devices were tiny, they could not be hidden there. However, he found that the hair or fur near the bottom of the mule's neck was so thick that he could easily install it under some perforated skin where it would not be noticed unless you were looking hard for it. In addition, it was because mules are so much smarter than horses, and he liked working with smarter animals.

"How do you know that?" Susan asked, with a smirk of disbelief.

"By their actions," Tom replied and continued, in an instructive tone, "If you put out food for a week, a horse will eat it all right away while a mule will eat what he needs and leave the rest for later. Also, if you have them hooked to a wagon, you can whip a horse and keep him going until he drops, but you cannot do that to a mule. When he gets tired, he stops, and there is nothing you can do that will make him go until he is rested. One day, long ago, a mule pulling a grocery wagon tied up traffic on Broad Street in Charleston for hours when he got tired."

"Wait, are you from Charleston, South Carolina?" Susan asks, as she rocks back in her chair.

"Yes, I am," Tom replied. "Why do you look so surprised?"

"So am I. Isn't that a coincidence!" she said.

"I worked with the Navy training dolphins before they moved their operation down to Florida. Now there's a smart animal. They are a lot smarter than mules."

"You mean you trained dolphins for the Navy? What was that all about?" she asked.

"Well, that's another long story." He signals to the waitress. "You should hold our orders and bring us a couple of martinis first."

Turning to Susan, he said, "This is one of my favorite stories. You'll like it."

"Back during the Cold War, the Navy came to me with a request to train a dolphin to pass a message by swimming into a submarine."

"How did you do that?"

"I didn't. I told them there was no way to train a dolphin to swim into a torpedo tube. They are too smart, and they would never swim into something that they could not turn around in."

"Why would the Navy want to do such a thing?"

"As I said, it was during the Cold War with Russia. Our Navy had developed a submarine that was so quiet they could sneak into a Russian harbor. The Navy quickly figured out it would be much more effective to bring two submarines in, but they would have to have some way to communicate without using radio or sonar."

"So, what did you do?"

"Nothing. I told them it was impossible and explained why. However, a couple of years later, they came back and said they had developed a sub with ballistic missile capability, and now they had a huge vertical launch tube that should accommodate a dolphin."

I said, "Okay, I would give it a try."

Susan just shook her head, exclaiming, "That's amazing. Training dolphins. I can hardly believe it."

Tom continued, "We taught the dolphin to swim in and out of the huge tube by attaching tiny bells onto the tips of his fins. Whenever he touched the inside of the tube, or silo as it is called, the bell would ring, and he would quickly manage to swim out of there. The impressive thing was that the dolphin was so smart that he could swim back in and try again, and after two or three tries, and never touched the wall again. Somehow, he had learned exactly how big the silo was."

"Wow, I guess dolphins really are smart."

"But the best part of the story is what happened in the Russian harbor," he continued.

"You mean they tried it? What happened?"

"It was a crazy accident. A training sub had a couple of sick sailors and was in a hurry to get back home, so they tried to combine two exercises: sneaking into a Russian harbor and cycling their dolphin in and out of their silo. It so happened that a Russian sub was submerged in that harbor and had its ballistic missile hatch open, so the dolphin made the mistake of swimming into the Russian silo.

Unfortunately, it was slightly smaller in diameter, and when the dolphin turned in the silo, he touched the wall, and the bell on his fin rang. It confused him so much that he made it ring several times before swimming out, and the Russians started yelling and cursing each other. We heard and recorded everything on our sonar, and some people in the Navy are still laughing about it. Here's lunch, just in time."

By that time, Susan was laughing so much that she could hardly eat lunch.

Walking back from lunch, they had a lot to discuss about Charleston. Susan's mother lives there, and she visits quite often. They found that they had both been to plays at the old Dock Street theater, praised the she-crab soup at 82 Queen Street restaurant, and argued about whether the service was better at Magnolia's or The Cotton Gin.

Refreshed, they returned to their working stations, each with another armload of files.

After only a few minutes, suddenly Susan sat up straight and announced, "I think I've found it! Just what we need! And they're mules, not horses!"

"That's even better. What did you find?"

"Listen to this. Two girls grew up together and rode horses and liked it so much that after they graduated from college, they took a trip out to the Grand Canyon and rode the mules down the dangerous path on the side of the canyon, a dream they both had as a graduation present. The mules they rode even had names, Ward and Heather. Can you imagine that? It was many years ago, but if we can find out where they are now, Hugh will be delighted!"

Susan passed the information to the FBI office about the two ladies she was looking for, and they put out an APB (all-points bulletin) to find them.

The traffic was heavy, and Susan was anxious to hurry back and tell Hugh all about it when her cell phone rang.

"Don't tell me you found them already. Really? That's fantastic! Yes, we are on our way now. He'll be delighted to hear it."

Turning to Tom, who was driving, she said, "We had fantastic luck. The APB was triggered immediately because one of the girls is married to an FBI agent, Jim Smithfield.

It's Kate. She is still a close friend of Jane's, although they live in different states and communicate regularly. We've got both addresses. I can't wait to tell Hugh about our luck."

"It wasn't all luck. We worked all afternoon to find it."

"That's true."

They drove into the CIA headquarters and went straight to Hugh's office.

 **CHAPTER FIVE**

Plan A

"You cannot believe what we found!" Susan beamed as she and Tom walked into Hugh's office.

"It must be something great since you are so excited. Did you find someone who owns a lot of horses and mules?"

"Better than that. We found two girls who rode mules down the steep trail into the Grand Canyon. The mules were named Ward and Heather. The girls are now grown women, and, get this, one of them is married to an FBI agent, Jim Smithfield. Not only that, we have their addresses for you. Their names are Jane Dogan and Kate Smithfield. Jane lives in North Carolina, and Kate lives in Florida, but they are life-long friends and are still in close contact with each other. It should be a perfect setup for your Deep Cover operation."

Hugh asked to see the two files and began to read. He noted that the files were about 20 years old when Jane and Kate were graduating from college. Susan's conversation with agent Smithfield revealed that Jane and Kate were always horse lovers as little girls. They grew up at the stables associated with their fathers' country club. While their friends were swimming or playing golf or tennis, Kate and Jane were at the stables either riding their horses or helping the management clean the stalls and other horses in order to be rewarded with extra free lessons. They were quite accomplished and competitive riders. They were rewarded athletic scholarships and were, with their horses, drafted into the school's equestrian team. This kept them focused on school and sports and kept them very physically fit. All of which ticked all the boxes for the FBI to watch them as candidates to be offered jobs after graduation.

"This looks very promising, indeed. They should fit perfectly into my Plan A," Hugh said as he continued to read.

The notes indicated that after graduation, and while the FBI was still following them and recording their activities, they made a trip to the Grand Canyon specifically to experience riding mules from the canyon's rim to its base.

When Hugh saw this, his eyebrow raised, and he nodded his head. The agent was even thorough enough to note in the file that Jane rode a mule named Ward and Kate rode a mule named Heather.

"That's perfect. You're right. It'll be an ideal way to use our Deep Cover operation. I am glad the agent keeping tabs on them was so thorough; little did anyone imagine that something seemingly insignificant in a file as a mule riding experience would cause candidates to be used later for Deep Cover to prevent suicide bombings in the United States.

Tom, please get on this right away and get those two mules rigged up with listening devices. The information about what those two men, Francois and Henri, were doing is just what I had suspected. They were trying to buy mules but had to lease them. The two mules will be shipped to Algiers. You need to get to those mules before they are shipped and install some listening devices. Later, after I've written some postcards, you'll need to go to Algiers and contact your local vets about those listening devices and what to do with the information. Of course, you will need to alert your other vets because they may transfer those mules to who knows where."

"Does this mean you will use your postcard method of message transmission with Deep Cover? If so, you better make a dry run to check it out." Tom suggested.

"Yes, that is my Plan A. You're right, and I will."

Tom left to make arrangements for his trip to Tusayan, Arizona, where the mules are.

 # CHAPTER SIX

Deep Cover

Susan has been listening to all this with rapt attention but a puzzled expression because she cannot understand what these postcards are all about. Finally, she can't hold back any longer.

"What in the world are these postcards all about?"

Hugh patiently explained, "It sounds mysterious, doesn't it? As it turns out, this will be the ideal occasion to keep everything secret and use our new message transmission system involving people under Deep Cover. Here's the situation: It is going to take the enemy at least a couple of months to recruit and train each new suicide bomber. We have enough agents in Europe so that all we need to know at the beginning is where they are going to obtain their recruits. A postcard arriving from that city will be the tip-off. The neat part that makes it such a secret is that the only message we are interested in is the stamp on the card that tells us what city it came from. We will have plenty of time to track what the enemy is doing, and the FBI will be ready to arrest him in this country when he arrives. The President will love you and the entire FBI for their wonderful work. You'll be my favorite heroine."

"That's a genius plan! I was told you were a genius before I met you. Now I really believe it!" Susan responded as she looked admiringly at Hugh.

"Well, thanks, but you should hold off your congratulations until our dry run proves effective. It will be up to you to get together with Jim Smithfield and explain the whole program to him. It will be vital to keep his wife and Jane under Deep Cover."

Susan said, "Wait a minute. What about those phones in your office; I thought that was your means of communication to the outside world."

"No, those are only for extreme emergencies. There are only four phones, and there are only eight CIA agents around the world cleared to use them. They would never be used for an ordinary CIA operation like this one."

"I'm amazed that you consider this an ordinary operation. I would also like to talk to you more about your ambitious plan for a College of Religions. I think I would like to be a part of it."

"There is nothing I would rather do than discuss it with you at length. How about dinner tonight?"

"That would be very nice. I'd love it."

Just then, Tom came back in with news he would be taking the evening flight out.

"Okay, Tom, it's time for you to go to the Grand Canyon and get those mules ready. Susan will put you in touch with her FBI agent there, who will know which mules and where and when they will be shipped to Algiers. The timing here works out perfectly because I am scheduled to meet with the President to give him an update on our progress tomorrow."

"Expect a call from me sometime tomorrow evening," Tom said as he left the room.

Hugh turned to Susan.

"I guess it's time for us to start writing some postcards to Jane. Just two or three from each of us will be enough for now."

"What are we going to say?"

"It doesn't make any difference what we say as long as it causes Jane to call her friend, Kate, and tell her where the card came from. I think the main key is to sign them from either mule, Ward, or Heather. That should do the trick."

"That sounds like fun."

"It will be. Make sure you use a different pen each time and try to use a different writing style so it will seem to come from a different person. We will give the cards to Tom when he comes back so he can take them to our agents in Europe."

"What are you going to tell the President when you meet with him tomorrow?"

"The only thing to tell the President is the absolute truth, including Plan A and all the details he asks for. He is a very straightforward, no-nonsense kind of guy and he will either approve what we are doing, make a constructive suggestion or say, "You are being replaced.""

Later, on the way home, Susan was preoccupied with reviewing everything that went on today. She said to herself, "I must sound like a gibbering idiot to Hugh. It seems like I cannot say anything to him without throwing the word 'love' in. I can't help it. Does it mean I am actually falling in love with him this quickly? I've never felt like this before and it really, really feels good. I feel like singing." She broke out into a loud chorus of "I'm sitting on top of the world," oblivious to the raised eyebrows of the car next to hers in the normal going-home traffic jam.

 # CHAPTER SEVEN

Ruth and Eve

Paris in the month of May is much like a hyperactive beehive with the usual throngs of enthusiastic visitors enjoying the cool, sunny weather. The streets are canopied with the lush blossoms of cherry trees and every spare space in front of each home and business is awash in bright colors of tulips, snapdragons, violets, and lilies.

Ruth and Eve had just graduated from the Universite' Paris Sud' which held their ceremony at the beautiful Hotel de Ville de Paris. It was, as always, dazzling with blooms of the season, making their infectious enthusiasm even brighter.

Ruth Cohen was a tall, dark-haired beauty with big brown eyes and a ready smile. As an only child, she followed in the footsteps of her father and studied architecture. Her father, Jacob Cohen, is probably the most prosperous architect in France, having made a name for himself through his devotion to his hero, Frank Lloyd Wright.

Eve, who has adopted the name Cohen, is a small, blue-eyed blonde, even prettier than Ruth if that is possible. She grew up with Ruth like a sister, having been taken in by the Cohens when she lost her parents in an automobile accident. They were both the same age, but Eve was the smarter of the two. She studied Business Administration, at the suggestion of Jacob who wanted them to work together for him without being competitive.

Following the ceremony, their father took them to Café de Musees for a lunch of various homemade pates accompanied by crispy French bread and a seasonal salad. Eve and Ruth sipped on wine and gave each other quick glances, attempting to contain their excitement as they ever-so-patiently waited for their father to say something about his oh-so secret graduation present to them.

"You can't believe how proud I am of both of you. I have both good news and bad news. Which would you like to hear first?" Jacob Cohen chided them.

"The good news, of course," they chirped in unison, bursting with anticipation.

"The good news is what you've always wanted, a trip to the United States with a vacation in Las Vegas, Nevada."

"Whoopee, you're right. That's exactly what we both wanted."

Eve eyed Mr. Cohen suspiciously, "What is the bad news, father?"

"The bad news is your freedom and fun are over. Now, you have to go to work and earn your own living. Since you will be working for me, that should be no problem. In fact, you will find out that in the U.S., that system is called 'a gravy train with biscuit-wheels.'"

"So, are you saying this trip will be a working vacation? There is no bad news in that. It sounds great," they both say excitedly.

"It may turn out to be much more than that. You may need to stay there for quite a while."

"This is starting to sound very intriguing," Ruth smiled at him in joking suspicion. "Tell us more about it."

"You remember reading about how some rich philanthropists like Warren Buffet are trying to improve the world by curing disease and various other things? Well, I have met a group like that here in France who have joined with some in the U.S.A. who want to improve the world with a different approach. Their reasoning is they can stop most wars from happening through education by teaching each religion enough about the others to create understanding and tolerance."

"How in the world do they plan on doing that?"

"The plan is to create a College of Religions. It will start by designing and building a Synagogue, a Mosque, and a Church next to each other where classes in each religion can be taught side-by-side. That's where you come in. The designs will have to be both alike and different so as not to offend anyone. That's why I was selected, because of my devotion to the architecture of Frank Lloyd Wright. They think we can do it."

"Why did they pick those three religions?" asked Ruth

"Because not only are they the three major religions by population, but their research showed that the religions of Judaism, Islam, and Christianity are called the Abrahamic Religions. All three pray to the same God. All three have shared beliefs, customs, and traditions, including that God made a covenant with Abraham. Also, they share the belief in the need to worship God in prayer and the recognition of personal and private prayer of each believer. They share in the common practice and tradition of giving charity as an act of kindness to help the poor, afflicted, aged, and widowed. All three also attach spiritual significance to water in various purification rituals. They also share in the concept of pilgrimage to holy sites where they seek forgiveness and strength in their connection with God. These holy sites may differ, but the core value is the same," explained Jacob.

"There must be more to this story," Eve wondered.

"There is. They already have the land to build it on. It is just outside of Las Vegas, Nevada."

"Oh, now we get the picture," another unison comment from his girls.

Jacob would have worried a little about the working gift, but he knew his daughters too well and knew their unison half-hearted admonishment was just a loving poke at him.

"Your mission in America will involve several things. In addition to establishing our new branch office in Las Vegas, you should learn all you can about the U.S.A. A long road trip to visit the best examples of Frank Lloyd Wright's designs will help you do that. It will involve going to New York, Chicago, Pittsburg, Racine, Wisconsin, Oak Park, Illinois, and Cloquet, Minnesota. In fact, since your plane goes through New York, you can start by staying over there for a couple of days to visit the museum there."

"It sounds like the first thing we will need to do there is to buy some comfortable shoes for all the walking we will be doing," Ruth said, holding out her hand to him for some cash.

"What in the world is in all those places you want us to visit?" Eve asked with a questioned look on her face. Ruth may be enthralled with all the architecture, but she was thinking of taking some side trips also.

"They are places that were designed by Frank Lloyd Wright. They are quite varied and will give you a broad knowledge of his thinking. It will take a lot of planning in order to make these three buildings both alike and separate. In New York, the place you will visit is the Guggenheim Museum. Then there is the Robie House at the University of Chicago, The Unity Temple at Oak Park, Illinois, the Johnson Wax Building in Racine, Wisconsin, a place called Falling Water near Pittsburg, Pennsylvania, and even a Phillips Gas

Station in Cloquet, Minnesota. When you have done all that, you should have learned enough about America to live there comfortably."

"That's fantastic! Even a gas station? Amazing! By the time we do all that traveling, we should feel at home in the United States."

"Yes, that's all part of the plan. I made reservations for you at the Paris Las Vegas Hotel. You should feel right at home there with the French food I am sure they will be serving in their dining room. After you have made your trip and gotten to know something about America, you should return to Las Vegas and find and lease a convenient place for our branch office. Here are your reservations and your airline tickets. You will be leaving early next week. You will notice there is a stopover in New York, so you can visit the Guggenheim Museum while you are there."

With a big smile on both of their faces, they replied, "Wow, you have thought of everything, Dad!" and, "All that extra time we spent in graduate school was really worth it!"

"Also, Ruth, here is my business card for you to use. After all, for my company, this is a business trip, but don't forget to have fun."

"You need not worry about that," they both chorused as they gave him a big hug.

"However, before you go, I want you to meet all nine of our philanthropists and their wives, if possible. I want to make sure they understand how we are going to establish this university of theirs. I will make the necessary appointments and take you both to meet them."

 **CHAPTER EIGHT**

The Meeting

As the flight approached New York, Ruth and Eve asked the stewardess if she knew what hotel would be close to the Guggenheim Museum and she said the only one she knew that would be within walking distance was The Franklin on 87th Street.

It was a long trip and they were tired so, after rounding up their luggage, they took a taxi directly to The Franklin and started their visit to New York with a nap.

The next morning, they had breakfast at the hotel and got directions from the waitress who called it the Solomon R. Guggenheim Museum. They walked three blocks down 87th Street and turned right to 89th Street where they stood in awe at the corner of 5th Avenue gaping at the beautiful round building which grew larger as it went up four rings.

"That is some building!" said Ruth.

"No wonder Dad admires Frank Lloyd Wright!" exclaimed Eve. "Let's go inside and look around."

They spent a couple of hours examining everything.

While Ruth and Eve were touring around New York, Francois and Henri were being instructed to leave Algiers to go to Las Vegas. Their flight changed planes in New York.

Algiers, the capital city of Algeria, is built on the slopes of the Sahal Hills, which parallel the Mediterranean Sea. As an ideal site for a military base, it had been over-thrown numerous times by various factions, the last being the French who dominated the Arab/Muslim inhabitants by pushing their culture on the people, improving and modernizing the infrastructure of Algeria, but sending its peoples, the native Muslim inhabitants, out of the cities to live in abject poverty working in unskilled labor jobs. It is no wonder that the rise to independence by the Algerians also led to Algeria becoming a haven for Muslim extremists. Through strife, a number of children became orphaned, both Muslim and French. Catholic Nuns in Algeria had turned their sanctuary into an orphanage and school as a result.

Francois and Henri were both orphans, brought up to the age of five in a Catholic orphanage in Algiers, where they were taught English by the Nuns in the hope of giving them a better chance to be adopted. They were so incorrigible that they were allowed to be adopted by a Muslim family who was anxious to give their only son playmates. A large donation to the orphanage helped allow the adoption. The Muslim family was one of the richest in Algeria, owning a number of oil wells. However, now, some twenty years later, the father had been killed in battle with Israel, and the only biological son, who insisted he be called the Boss, was intent on seeking revenge by recruiting and training suicide bombers.

Francois had grown up to be over six feet tall, a handsome young man with black hair and a beard, while his friend, Henri was blond with blue eyes and only five feet six inches tall. They both had become fluent in English, French, and Arabic and were currently language teachers at the University of Algiers. Both felt a brotherly attachment to the Boss, having grown up with him.

The Boss was obsessed with the idea of moving his secret meetings in Algiers to a location inaccessible to potential eavesdroppers.

He told Francois and Henri that he had found the ideal place for his secret meetings which was on the side of a mountain that could be reached only on horseback although it was a dangerous path. In any case, he had been thrown from a horse twice and would not get on one again. A stable nearby had mules but they were only pack-animals, never broken to be ridden. He learned that well-trained mules were used for tourists to ride down into the Grand Canyon in the United States and it would be perfect if he could buy six of them and have them shipped to Algiers.

He made arrangements for Francois and Henri posing as French tourists, to fly from Algiers to Las Vegas with a change of planes in Paris and again in New York. He gave them their passports, Francois Allard and Henri Blanchet, and a money belt each, instructing them to pay cash only and wire him for a money transfer once they made their deal for the mules. He told them not to call him but to write him a letter each day and not to leave the letter for someone else to mail, but to put it in the mailbox themselves.

As luck would have it, Ruth and Eve were flying first class on the same plane out of New York to Las Vegas and as Francois and Henri walked past them to their seats in coach, Eve elbowed Ruth to look at the two handsome young men who just boarded the plane.

After landing in Las Vegas, they waited for their luggage and saw the same young men looking at them across the carousel. They each gave a quick smile to the other as they picked out their luggage and found themselves thrown together again while they waited for the shuttle bus to the Paris Las Vegas hotel.

Eve, the more outgoing of the two, decided to strike up a conversation.

"Obviously, we are both staying at the Paris Las Vegas hotel. Are you from France too?"

Francois quickly and easily responded in French, "Sort of. We got on the plane in Paris and had to change planes in New York. You sound French too. Have you been in New York long?"

"No. We just stopped over for a short time. We are on a traveling vacation. How about you?"

"We are trying to mix a little business with pleasure as tourists," Francois replied.

They chatted back and forth during the ride about the weather and the sights of all the neon signs; all, that is, except Henri who was nervous and very quiet. He was surprised they had met anyone so quickly. He wanted to do the job of getting those mules for the Boss quickly and get back home before anyone found out who they really were.

There was no mistaking the Paris hotel built with a nod to Versailles in style with the Eiffel tower proudly replicated in front. Eve and Ruth couldn't wait to see what the hotel had to offer.

As the bus pulled into the hotel, Francois, ever the romantic and completely drawn to Ruth, worried that, due to the enormity of the hotel, they may never see these ladies again. Abruptly he turned to Ruth and said, "How about joining us for dinner? I understand there is a great restaurant on the roof of this hotel. We wouldn't even have to go out."

Ruth smiled, hoping he didn't notice her little sigh of relief that he asked, and replied quickly for both of them, "We would be delighted! It will take a while for us to change and get more presentable. After we check in, I will give you our room number and you can stop by around 7:00 o'clock."

Once checked in, they realized their rooms were in different directions so they headed off to their respective elevators after confirming the dinner date.

"What a beautiful hotel! I wonder what the Boss would think if he saw this. Do you think he realizes how expensive this place must be?" said Francois.

"It makes me nervous just to think about the Boss," replied Henri.

"Weren't we lucky meeting those two beautiful French girls here in the USA? I would sure like to get to know them better," Francois thought aloud.

Francois opened the door to their room and walked in, happy there were two queen-sized beds. He chose the one closest to the window and opened the curtain. "What a view!" he looked out at the Eiffel tower and a good portion of the Las Vegas strip. "Wow, this is going to be a great trip; I can feel it!" he says.

"Seriously, Henri, I really would like to get to know Ruth better. What about you?"

Henri flopped down on the other bed and finally felt more at ease. He sighed, "Me too. It's too bad we can only be here a short time. We have to get those mules for the Boss and get out of here before anyone finds out who we are. Why isn't he satisfied with horses anyhow?"

"He's been thrown from a horse twice. Besides, mules are much more sure-footed and can go where horses cannot."

"It's not going to be much fun as a tourist if we really have to stay out of the casinos," Henri grumbled.

"That's true, but we can't afford to be photographed by all those cameras they have. Maybe we'll have to depend on the girls to have some fun."

"Well, I'm sure looking forward to seeing Eve again at dinner. However, I'm worried. Don't you think it a little odd that they happened to get on our plane in New York?"

"Henri, why must you be so suspicious? If you don't relax a little, others might become suspicious of us," Francois admonished. "They explained that they had just stopped over to visit New York for a couple of days as part of their vacation."

"I hope they are as innocent as they seem. It's almost too good to be true. It wouldn't surprise me a bit if they turned out to be FBI Agents."

"Pfft," Francois snorted. "Get dressed and get in a better mood."

Ruth and Eve were booked into a beautiful suite on the 25th floor. They walked into a sitting room with two love seats that faced each other. A large screen TV hung on one side of the room and a wet bar on the other. The back of the room was completely glassed in with a long but narrow balcony on the other side. To the left and right of them were bedroom areas also complete with TVs and an individual bath for each.

"Wow. Dad went all out when he booked us into this room! This is a far better place than the place we stayed in, in New York! From what I can see, everything in Las Vegas is bigger and more over-the-top than anywhere else."

Ruth was walking back and forth trying to decide which room to take when Eve jumped in and made the decision for her.

"Before we unpack," she chimed, "let's just sit in this glorious suite for a minute and take it all in, shall we?"

Eve curled up on one of the love seats and gazed out the large sliding glass doors.

Ruth poured them both a glass of wine from the minibar and sat opposite her.

"What do you think of Henri? Isn't he the cutest thing?" Eve gushed.

"He's okay but too short for me to dance with," Ruth commented, as she swirled the wine in her glass.

"You mean you are thinking of dancing with him already?"

"No, I'm thinking of not dancing with him. I sure would like to dance with Francois, though. He is really my type," Ruth said with a heavy sigh.

After a glass of wine each, Eve noticed the clock on the wall. "We better get ready. They are supposed to pick us up for dinner soon."

They headed off to their respective bedrooms to unpack and freshen up. At precisely 7:00, there was a knock on the door.

"I'll get it," called Ruth as Eve was still in her room, primping.

She opened the door and again took in just how handsome Francois was.

He thought his jaw was going to drop when he saw Ruth in a stunning sapphire blue dress that clung to her figure in all the right places.

"Come on in," she said, very off-handedly, apparently unaware of her effect on him. "Eve will be right out."

They sat on the love seats, Francois and Henri on one and Ruth on the other with her back toward Eve's room.

"We confirmed that there is a great French restaurant right here on the roof of the hotel and have a reservation for 7:30," Francois said, enthusiastically.

"Yes, but don't you want to go down to the casino first and try our luck?" Ruth asked, hopefully.

"No, we promised our Boss we would avoid the temptations of the casinos while we are here on his nickel," Francois explained.

"That's too bad. You might find some other temptations if you look around a little bit," Ruth kidded.

"I like your attitude," Francois said, ready to start flirting back when Eve entered the room.

He and Henri immediately sprang to their feet. She was stunning with her long blonde hair pulled back in a French braid with just a few wisps of hair framing her face. The soft orange silk of her slip dress set off the French Riviera tan on her model slim figure.

"Wow!" was all Henri could muster.

"Well, thanks for that," Eve said as she smiled at Henri. "I hope I look alright. I'm a little jet-lagged, but I think getting out and about will pick me back up."

"By the way, tomorrow we are going to drive out to visit the Grand Canyon. Maybe you would like to come along. It's a long way there, so it might be an overnight trip," Francois suggested.

"That might be rushing it a little bit. We plan to start by doing some shopping. We are going to look for a couple of pairs of mules," Eve replied.

Francois and Henri froze and stared at each other, both wondering if Henri's suspicion was correct. Finally, Francois stammers, "Where would you go in Las Vegas to buy mules?"

"Why, to a shoe store, of course."

"They sell mules in shoe stores?"

"Yes, they are very comfortable shoes, ideal for all the walking we plan to do while sight-seeing."

Francois and Henri's faces both relaxed as they learn that mules are also a type of shoe. Henri rolled his eyes and, with a slight sigh of relief, said, "Well, we better head out. We have reservations."

As the ladies go out the door, Henri pulled Francois back and whispers, "Be careful. They still might be FBI!"

The rooftop bar offered a stunning view of Las Vegas. The neon lights of the hotels provided a breathtaking view. No one was very hungry, so they ordered drinks and four different appetizers to share. A band was playing on the far side of the room, and when they started a slow song, Francois and Henri asked the girls to dance. When Ruth's hand touched Francois, and his hand slipped around her waist, she felt like she had known him forever. They moved so easily together, swaying to the music as they moved slowly around the dance floor. Neither said a word. They just smiled at each other. She put her head on his shoulder and closed her eyes. He held her closer, hoping the song would never end. Henri and Eve were not as comfortable with each other. Henri was still somewhat suspicious at their fortune of bumping into these girls, and Eve kept looking at him with an inquisitive smile.

"What's on your mind, gorgeous?" he asked, trying to sound relaxed.

"It's just that when I look at you, I seem to see my face looking back at me," she said, a little embarrassed to let that thought slip out.

"Oh, please tell me I don't have such a feminine face," he pleaded.

"No, it's not that. It's just that we both are blonde. We have blue eyes and yours seem to be the same shape as mine. Even your nose seems to be the same shape. It's almost like I am looking at a long-lost brother," she said. "Geez, I hope not!"

He laughed and felt a little more at ease with her answer than what he was afraid she might say.

Wanting to stay and enjoy each other's company, they continued to have a few more drinks, some more dances, dessert, and, finally, a nightcap before heading back down to the girls' suite.

 # CHAPTER NINE

Two Mules

The next day Francois and Henri took a taxi back to the airport where they could rent a car. On the way, they reminded each other not to mention to anyone that they were here on business. They should be careful to remember that they were just tourists from France.

At the car rental counter, Francois said to the lady rental agent, "We would like to rent a car, please," as he presented her with his driver's license and his passport.

She handed him back his passport, saying, "I won't need this. How long would you want the car for?"

"I'm not sure," he said, "We are just tourists from France visiting the Grand Canyon and we would like to drive out to a town called Tusayan where we have hotel reservations."

"Well, that means you would probably need it for two or three days. Do you know how to get there?"

"Maybe it would be better if you showed us," he replied.

She reached under the counter and came up with a map of Arizona. She unfolded it, turned it, and laid it on the counter so they could read it. Pointing to the route, she said, "You need to take route 93, which will take you through Boulder City to cross the Hoover Dam. By the way, since you apparently haven't been here before, you would probably enjoy stopping at the dam and taking the tour through it. It's very interesting. Then you will continue down route 93 to Kingman, then across Interstate 40 to Williams and turn North on state road 64 to Tusayan."

After Francois and Henri had left, she turned to another agent and said, "Wasn't that odd? Did you notice that?"

"What?"

"That customer. He said they were *just* tourists. A lot of people have told me they were tourists, but he was the first person I ever heard say *just* tourists."

CHAPTER TEN

Tusayan, Arizona

During the trip, Francois and Henri were deeply impressed by the United States. They found the freedom to be almost unbelievable. Just crossing the state line without having to stop and show their passports was quite a shock. When they reached the Hoover Dam, they followed the agent's suggestion to take the tour. Afterward, they went into the gift shop to search for any and everything they could find about the United States. They bought a map of the United States together with a couple of geography books so they could study the country.

Just before entering Tusayan, Arizona where their hotel was, Henri looked to the left of the road and exclaimed, "Look at that, a small airport right here. We could have flown here instead of this long car drive."

"Yes, but think of all the sights we would have missed. We would have never seen the Hoover Dam, for instance," countered Francois.

"You're right. You can learn a lot more by driving than by flying," agreed Henri.

After checking in at the hotel and getting to their room, Francois made a couple of phone calls and set up a meeting the next morning to talk about buying some mules. Apparently, the mules that people rented to ride down the trail into the canyon were all owned by a man named John Smith.

The next morning, they met with John Smith. Mr. Smith looked exactly like what they pictured a cowboy to be, dressed in a cowboy hat, tee shirt, jeans, chaps, and boots. He was leaning against the corral, chewing on a piece of hay and looking at his livestock.

Francois, who wanted to get the business over with quickly approached Mr. Smith and said, "We are very interested in your mules and would like to buy some. How many do you have?"

"Not enough. They are not easy to train. But I am getting some more. They are not for sale," he replied.

Mr. Smith spat on the ground. He didn't seem too friendly and certainly not open to selling.

Francois and Henri looked at each other. Henri turned to Mr. Smith and said, "Look, we badly need at least two of your mules. We haven't even talked about a price. I know they are very valuable. How much will you take for just two of them?"

John Smith just shook his head, smiling, and said, "You don't understand. It takes a lot of time to train these mules and I never have enough of them. If I started selling them, I would go out of business. It takes at least a month just to break them in for someone to ride them. It's much harder than a horse. Then they have to learn the trail. Then they have to learn to let strangers ride them, a different stranger each time. I wouldn't think of selling any of them."

Francois and Henri start talking to each other in French, "What are we going to do? We can't go home empty-handed!"

John Smith shrugged his shoulders and started to walk away.

"Wait, no, come back, please," Francois pleaded.

"Let's try to work something out," Henri added.

"Maybe we can lease them."

John stopped, turned around slowly, and said, "Alright, you sound desperate. Where did you say you are from?"

"Algeria," they both say in unison.

"I'll tell you what I can do. There is a stable in Algeria that I have done business with in the past. I can lease two mules to you and ship them to that stable. You will have to keep them there when you are not riding them and let the people in that stable take care of them and send them back to me after three months only. But it will be expensive," John said.

"That's fine," Francois replies, "We expected it to be expensive. When can you send them?"

"It will be at least three weeks before I can let them go. Will that be satisfactory?"

They both nod their heads vigorously, saying, "That will be fine."

Francois and Henri return to their hotel, exhausted but happy and greatly relieved.

Henri found and raided the mini-bar and made himself comfortable. Francois made himself a drink and unpacked the information about the U.S. They started to learn all they could about the United States, intending to prove to the Boss that they were experts on the subject when they got back.

Francois said, "I can understand why Boss hates Israel for killing his father during the war. But to extend that hatred to Israel's allies and friends is a very foolish thing to do."

"I agree with you one hundred percent. We've got to find some way to persuade him otherwise."

They marveled over facts like the tiny state of Vermont being larger than Israel. Francois pointed out to Henri that if a cutout of the United States were laid over Europe, it would cover all of Europe, including the Mediterranean Sea.

"We have to write the Boss and tell him all about this. The Boss knows this country is an ally of Israel. Why does he want to be their enemy?" asks Henri. "I would certainly want to be their friend. Are you sure you want to go back?

"It wouldn't take much for Ruth to persuade me to stay and find a job here," Francois said.

Now that they had time on their hands waiting for the mules to be shipped, they decided it would be ideal if Ruth and Eve invited them to learn more about the country by joining them on their trip to Minnesota and Pennsylvania

 # CHAPTER ELEVEN

The Four Become Acquainted

Eve and Ruth spent a leisurely morning shopping and strolling around the Las Vegas strip. Finally, somewhat tired and definitely hot, they decided to spend the rest of the afternoon poolside.

Eve had seemed overly quiet during the afternoon and Ruth chalked it up to jet lag.

After coming back to their suite, she became concerned when she saw Eve pacing the floor with a frown on her face and slowly shaking her head.

"What's the matter, Eve? You look like you've lost your last friend," said Ruth, sympathetically.

"I'm thinking about Henri and how I feel about him. I'm almost afraid to spring my DNA testing on him. It's quite a quandary," she says, with a little moan.

For years, she had been searching for a living relative. She had even gone so far as to subscribe to a DNA searching service that has supplied her with a kit to gather DNA samples and have them analyzed. Now, she is afraid of what the result will be if she gets a sample from Henri and it turns out positive. She quickly developed strong feelings for Henri the first time she saw him but not a sisterly feeling, far from it. Pensively, she asks Ruth, "Do you think Henri looks like me?"

Ruth smiled. She knew exactly what Eve was thinking. "Well, he does have blue eyes and blond hair, much like yours. But he looks way too masculine to look anything like you. Are you going to test every blue-eyed blonde we find in America?"

"No, you are right; there should be more of a connection. They will be by in a few minutes to take us to dinner. It will be a good opportunity to get to know them better," she thought aloud.

As they walked down to Ruth and Eve's room, Henri asked Francois, "Did you find a nice restaurant off the strip where we can take them for dinner without the prying eyes of surveillance cameras?"

"Sure did," Francois replied as he knocked on the door. He was greeted by Ruth.

"I've rented a car," Francois started, "and found a place where the locals eat. Are you up for an adventure?"

"Sure," Ruth and Eve chimed in unison. "Let's go."

As they drove towards the restaurant, Francois pulled into a nondescript strip mall in Las Vegas' China Town.

"Here we are, hope you like Japanese grill-type food," Francois said excitedly.

They sat down and ordered Raku's Tofu as an appetizer. Kobe Beef, Apple Marinated Lamb Chops, and Duck with Balsamic Soy Sauce.

The restaurant had tall backed booths that gave a cozy, intimate feel which made Eve comfortable enough to ask, "This is our second dinner date. Do you mind if we ask you some personal questions?"

Henri pops up, "As long as you let us ask some too."

He had been worried that they were FBI agents and was still very suspicious of how they met. "Let me ask you this. Obviously, you are French. You had mentioned that you were visiting New York from France. Why did you leave New York to come to Las Vegas?"

"We had stopped over in New York to see a building designed by Frank Lloyd Wright at my father's suggestion. It was just pure coincidence that we came to Las Vegas on the same plane with you," Ruth said straightforwardly as she reached for a piece of tofu.

Henri said, "Really? You stopped to see a building? What are you, an architect or something?"

"Exactly, I am a newly graduated architect and my dad is one of the most famous architects in France, Mr. Cohen. Surely you have heard of him," Ruth said as she crinkled her face, not sure if she liked the tofu.

"Cohen? Does that mean he is Jewish?"

"Yes, is that a problem?"

"No, no that is not a problem. It's just a surprise. Eve is the first blue-eyed, blonde Jewish girl I have ever seen."

Henri was getting more suspicious and trying not to let it show.

"Well, she is not really my sister."

Henri's eyebrows shoot up and he glances over at Francois who nods slowly to him, obviously suspicious.

"She just came to live with us when her parents passed away. We grew up together just like sisters," Ruth replied in a dismissive, unsuspecting fashion. "What part of France are you two from?"

Henri sighs clamps his lips together with a little smile and bobs his head seeming to be satisfied with that explanation.

"We don't know," Francois was almost apologetic. "We grew up in a Catholic orphanage in Algiers and were five years old when we were both adopted together with two other boys by a Muslim family."

"Wait a minute; you say you were brought up in a Catholic orphanage and were adopted by a Muslim family?" Ruth was now intrigued. "How could that be? You have French names."

Henri again, started to really get worried about all this information coming out and tried, unsuccessfully, to kick Francois under the table. However, Francois, being quick-witted, quickly covered it up by saying, "The Nuns had already taken care of that by giving us last names. They were trying to make us more easily adopted by French, British, or even American candidates before we outgrew the orphanage. After all, we were already five years old."

He said all that glibly as Henri relaxed, both knowing that they would have to live with those fake passports and driver's licenses which Boss had provided.

Francois, who did not share Henri's suspicious nature, opened up. "I know it sounds strange and maybe it is but, that's what happened. We later learned the story. The Muslim family had three girls and finally a boy, who we call Boss. They lived out in the country where their oil wells were and Boss had no other children to play with. One day the father came home and found the four children playing together and the girls had dressed the little boy up like another girl. The father was furious. He said he would fix that problem right away and he did. He searched everywhere for boys to adopt and finally found us and two others in the Catholic orphanage.

We were all about the same age and a couple of years younger than Boss. He made a very generous contribution to the orphanage and offered to take all four of us. The orphanage was somewhat reluctant having spent a great effort teaching us English and French in addition to Arabic in the hope of finding suitable parents in either France or England. However, the combination of a large amount of money plus the fact that we were raising enough chaos to drive the Nuns up the wall, won Mother Superior over. She exacted the promise from him that he would send us all to college and that is how Henri and I became language professors."

"That's an amazing story," Ruth exclaimed. "How old were you when you were adopted?"

"We were both five," Francois replied.

"By that time, the Nuns must have instilled some Catholic teaching into you both," Eve suggested.

"Yes, they had," Francois replied. Turning to Henri, he said, "Do you remember the story about the ants?"

"You mean the time they brought us all into the kitchen?" Henri asked.

"Yes, one of the Nuns called several of us together and told us to come into the kitchen; there was something important she wanted us to see. She showed us some ants and said, 'Do you see those ants? Suppose you wanted to talk to them and tell them something. How could you do it? You couldn't. It would be impossible, right?'"

"Of course," they all chorused.

"You would have to change yourself into an ant, right? Well, that's what God did. He changed himself into a baby in Mary's womb and came down to tell us many things; the main thing was that we should love each other."

They all four sat silently for a moment, deep in thought and looking from one to another.

Finally, Ruth broke the silence by saying, "It sounds like your adopted Father made good on his promise. Language professors are sought after all over the world these days." She took another bite of duck, "It's fun to share plates of food like this. It feels more intimate. More familiar. More relaxed. "She stammered at the end of her sentence, surprised and embarrassed that the word 'intimate' rolled so quickly and sensuously off her tongue.

She quickly talked on, changing the subject, "Eve was orphaned too and believed she may have a sibling that she has never met. Henri, the two of you look so much alike. Would you mind doing a DNA test?"

Eve, surprised by Ruth's forwardness, went with it and dug into her purse for the cotton swabs, test tubes, caps, and stick-on labels.

"It's a simple thing. Do you mind?" Eve pleaded with Henri batting her beautiful blue eyes at him and smiling her best, irresistible smile.

"Wait a minute!" Henri exclaimed. Now he was getting even more suspicious. "What is this all about? I don't want to know who my parents are. Forget it!"

In an attempt to calm Henri down and not ruin their evening, Ruth sweetened her voice as if talking to a child, "No, this is not to find your parents. This is just to find out if you are related to Eve. You wouldn't want to be kissing your sister, would you?"

Eve looked pleading at Henri again. Henri raised his eyebrows and looked at Francois hoping for some help.

"I don't see how it could hurt any of us to learn if we are related in any way. I think Ruth and I should join you both in this interesting experiment," Francois volunteered.

Henri dropped his head, dejected and feeling very much alone in this discussion. "Oh, alright," he conceded. "Let's get it over with."

Eve just laughed and passed out the equipment. Everyone swabbed their mouth and assembled the test tube packages with labels.

"How long does it take to get the answers?" Henri asked meekly, as he felt himself melting into her beautiful eyes.

"Sometimes it takes days and sometimes weeks. We just have to be patient and wait."

"Well, it better come out right because I can tell you right now, if I had a sister there is no way I could feel this way about her," Henri insisted.

Eve had a big, satisfied grin on her face as she wrapped everything all up for mailing and they continued to chat and enjoy the meals set before them.

During dinner, Ruth explained their trip plans and why her father wanted them to visit the sites of several of Frank Lloyd Wright's building designs.

Shyly she asked Francois, "Do you have to return to Algiers soon? It would be such an adventure for you to accompany us on our trip."

"We may not need to go back so soon," Francois replied as he winked at Henri. "We would certainly take any opportunity we could to see more of this country. How about we call it an early evening so we can make a few calls from our hotel room?"

"That would be fine," Ruth said. "Our flight doesn't leave until later in the afternoon so there will be plenty of time to add the two of you in the morning if you are able to make the trip with us. I think Eve and I would both feel a little safer traveling across the country accompanied by two handsome men."

Her voice came out in a sultry tone, that both she and Francois blushed a little. Henri and Eve looked at each other with satisfied smiles.

Ruth was a little disappointed that they were not going to spend another night dancing in each other's arms, but the prospect of the trip now gave the whole evening a satisfying glow.

 # CHAPTER TWELVE

Tourists

As they left the restaurant and headed back to the hotel, they talked about all the places they planned to visit, staying for a few days in each, and what fun it would be to be all together on such an adventure. Francois commented that they had not, financially, planned on staying that long and didn't know about wiring money from Algiers.

Ruth frowned and thought for a minute, then said, "I will tell you what we can do. My dad gave me his business credit card to pay for everything that he had not already arranged for us. Since this is a business trip, I can put everything on his credit card and if he gets upset about it, you both can pay him back once the trip is over."

"Let me make some phone calls first," Francois said and gave her a kiss on the cheek as he let her out of the car.

Once back in their room, Henri worried, "What about the Boss? What are we going to tell him?"

Francois considered this and then said, "We will just write him each day as he instructed but first, I need to convince him that it will be in his best interest for us to tour the United States and we have found two ladies who are willing to pay for us to travel with them so there should be no way to trace our whereabouts and we will be learning all we can about the United States. The knowledge we will gain on this trip should be of benefit to him and his decisions going forward."

With that, Francois made the phone call. Henri paced the floor while Francois spoke to the Boss. After what seemed like an eternity, Francois hung up and said, "It's all set! We can go! Do you think it's too late to call the girls?"

Henri was so relieved he was grinning from ear to ear. He replied, "No, it's not too late. Go ahead and call their room and let them know."

Ruth hung up from talking to Francois and turned to Eve, "They are coming with us!" she said with delight. I just know this is going to turn out to be a wonderfully romantic trip. Francois said that he and Henri needed to do some shopping for additional clothes and would meet us here in the afternoon so we could take a taxi together to the airport."

Eve fell back on her bed, arms outstretched, and stared at the ceiling, "This is turning into so much fun! I can't wait to get the results of the DNA tests back so I will be more at ease with Henri!"

"I will call the airline right now and add two more to our flight to Duluth, Minnesota," Ruth said excitedly as she picked up the phone to make the arrangements.

The next morning, they packed, checked out precisely at 11:00, explaining to the desk clerk that they would all four be back in about ten days and would like the same rooms when they return, and had an early lunch at a restaurant in the hotel and waited in the lobby for Francois and Henri to arrive.

They walked in a little past 2:00, bags in hand. Francois immediately walked up, and as if they had been dating for years, gave Ruth a hello kiss while Henri picked up Eve's bag also and went out to have the Bellman hail a cab.

On the way to the airport, they held hands and kept looking at each other and smiling. Neither could make small talk, but that was okay, they were comfortable just being together.

Once at the airport, the clerk advised that the two first class seats that were originally booked were, of course, still available; but the later booking of two additional seats were only available in coach. Since they are going to have dinner on the flight, Francois and Henri insisted that the ladies take the first-class seats.

As soon as they got settled in, Eve pulled the airline magazine out of the pocket of the seat in front of her and asked Ruth where she thought they ought to stay on their first night.

"Well, that's a good question, since I'm going to be paying for it. I don't think any large hotel would have any objection as long as we insist on two separate rooms, not connecting. See what you can find in that magazine."

While perusing the magazine, Eve exclaimed, "Wow! Look at this!" she elbowed Ruth to get her attention. "It's a hotel designed specifically to accommodate eloping couples! Can you imagine that?" she handed the magazine to Ruth.

Admiring the picture of the 1908 Italian Renaissance design of the mansion and carriage house and looking over the advertisement, she shook her head and responded, "You're right," says Ruth, nodding her head. "This is amazing. Cotton Mansion offers several unique elopement packages. Let's file this away for future reference. However, it's much too early for this kind of talk."

"Yes, I agree. But doesn't it sound nice?"

"Yes, very nice, but don't get carried away. Remember, you had Henri take the DNA test and we don't have the results and won't for some time," Ruth responded.

Eve sighed and went back to flipping through her magazine.

Ruth settled back and closed her eyes, thinking it was a good time for a nap. Just as she started to doze off the stewardess arrived at her elbow to ask what they would like to drink.

Back in coach, Francois opened the newspaper that he picked up hurriedly as they walked through the airport terminal. Reading the headline "Captured Suicide Bomber" he sat bolt upright and in a hushed voice, speaking French instead of English, so as not to be overheard, he said, "Look at this, Henri. The FBI caught this guy who tried to blow up an airplane with a bomb in his shoe. Isn't that the guy, the Boss and his group, went to London to train?"

Henri's eyes opened as big as saucers. He leaned over, close to Francois, and whispered in French, "If it is, he was never supposed to get to the United States. The bomb was supposed to go off in the plane before it got here. I'm sure glad the Boss didn't get us involved in that. I wonder what happened."

Henri turned away, a frown on his face as he looked out the window for a minute. Finally, he turned back to Francois and continued whispering, "Our problem is, if anyone is able to tie that guy to the Boss, they'll be able to become suspicious of us. This traveling by air is beginning to get pretty scary. We could get off a plane somewhere and find the FBI waiting there for us. Let's see if we can get Ruth and Eve to switch to a rental car for the rest of the trip. Since Ruth seems to be calling the shots, why don't you try to talk her into it? She seems very taken with you."

"That's a good idea," Francois continued. "We would get to see a lot more of the country too. This flying high above it doesn't do much for me. I wonder what they're talking about. I hope they don't have a newspaper. Let's throw this one away and try not to talk about the subject."

Henri, a bit more serious, looked sternly at Francois, "We'll just keep calm and play ignorant of the Boss and anything he does. Remember, we are just tourists from Paris. There is no reason to suspect us of anything. Leasing those mules at the whim of the Boss is all we came for. There is nothing illegal in that. Besides, traveling around the country with those two beautiful girls provides great cover unless, of course, it turns out they are with the FBI."

Francois sat back a little questioning Henri again, "You don't still think that's a possibility, do you?"

"No, I guess not. It still seems like a miracle that we met them and found them so friendly, though," Henri said more to try to assure himself than Francois.

Francois took a deep breath, "I'm pretty close to falling in love. Look down at that countryside. I'm still amazed at how big this country is. We could see a lot more of it riding in a car."

"When we think they have finished dinner, I'll go up and ask Eve to change seats with me. Then I'll propose that we switch to a rental car in Duluth for the rest of the trip."

"That's a good idea; oh look, here comes Eve now."

Immediately, Francois stood to give her his seat and walked up to first class to join Ruth. Henri took Eve's hand as they gazed into each other's eyes like a couple of love-sick puppies.

"You know, Henri," Eve stated, "I am starting to regret asking you to take the DNA test. I am so drawn to you. I don't usually feel such a strong connection so quickly."

"I know. I feel the same way," Henri replied, "but since we did, let's just enjoy each other's company until we find out."

"Agreed. How about a game of cards to pass the time? I have a complimentary deck from the hotel. Black Jack or Gin?"

 **CHAPTER THIRTEEN**

Escapade

"Did you have a nice dinner, Ruth?" Francois asked, sliding into the seat next to her.

"Yes, we did. How about you?"

"We did. It was better than I expected. We have been talking about the trip and thinking we would learn a lot more about the U.S.A. if we were in a car instead."

"Eve and I were thinking the same thing. Long distance flying gets kind of boring after a while, doesn't it? Although our plane reservations take us all the way to Duluth, this plane doesn't go there, you know. We have to stop in Minneapolis and change planes.

The town we are going to, Cloquet, is on the road between Minneapolis and Duluth. It seems like it would make more sense to deplane in Minneapolis, cancel our flight reservation to Duluth and rent a car."

"That sounds fine to me. I will be glad to do some of the driving if you don't mind."

"That's fine.

 # CHAPTER FOURTEEN

Lost

Hugh and Susan, trying to figure out whether Francois and Henri are a threat to National Security, are getting late information from the FBI on their whereabouts. They only just learned that they flew out with Ruth and Eve to Duluth, Minnesota, and are somewhat perplexed.

"Maybe Francois and Henri are just tourists after all and have nothing to do with Boss and his terrorism campaign," Susan commented to Hugh as she hoped for the best.

"On the other hand, maybe Ruth and Eve are also working for Boss and these four people are up to no good," Hugh replied, ever the skeptic when it came to international terrorism.

They decided that the only course was to assume the worse and let the FBI continue to watch whatever they were doing.

Hugh mentioned that before there was a Global Positioning System that he used to collect maps. He moved over to his filing cabinet, opened a drawer, and started thumbing through a bunch of state maps until he found one of Minnesota. Taking the map over to his desk and unfolding it he motioned Susan over.

Concerned, Susan says, "I hate to tell you but we have no FBI office in Duluth."

"Really? That's interesting. Where is the nearest office?"

"Minneapolis."

"You better call and have them send an agent to Duluth. We'll have to follow them until we figure out what they are up to. Let's review what we know. Correct me if I miss something.

"They came from Algiers via Paris, tried to buy mules, and finally were allowed to lease only two to be sent to a rental stable in Algiers. We are sure they are somehow tied to and probably working for a man called 'Boss' that was responsible for recruiting and training at least one suicide bomber which we now have in custody. They acted like tourists and now, suddenly, they are acting like tourists again."

He and Susan leaned over the open map on the desk to study it. Susan suddenly pointed and said, "There, just north of Duluth, is a place called French River. Maybe, that's where they are headed."

"I doubt it. That seems too obvious. But you may as well mention it to your agent."

The FBI agent in Minneapolis headed to the Duluth airport. He checked with the airline and found out that the people he was interested in canceled their reservations to Duluth. He notified his FBI office in Minneapolis to have another agent sent to the airport to check all the rental car companies.

Sure enough, Ruth Cohen had rented a black, Ford Hybrid from the Enterprise Rental agency with the understanding that she could turn it in at any one of their offices. He asked if she was going to Duluth and the clerk said that she had no idea where she was going but that credit card, she was using could take them anywhere. She said it was a French credit card with enough credit that she could have bought a car for each of them if she wanted to. She went on to say that even with that big credit rating she was a very frugal person because she insisted on renting a hybrid for its great gas mileage even waiting for one to be available.

Hugh hated waiting around for information. Feeling a little antsy about having lost track of their potential targets, he felt he had to let off some steam. "I'm going to the driving range and hit some balls for about an hour," he said to Susan. "Do you play golf?"

"That is the one thing I never tried before," she replied. "But can I go with you and watch? I hate sitting around the office waiting to hear something back and I am sure we won't hear anything for a few hours."

"Sure, why not?" Hugh said. "Maybe I'll even let you take a whack at a few. I think you will find it very cathartic."

Luckily, Susan was wearing slacks and had a pair of running shoes in the car so she grabbed them before joining Hugh.

On the way to the driving range, he asked Susan if she played any sports that involved eye-hand coordination and she confirmed that she had been an avid tennis player in her teens and played a little girl's fast-pitch softball with her college sorority, but that was it.

At least she had a concept of eye-hand coordination, Hugh thought. He bought a large bucket of balls and pulled several clubs out of his golf bag which he left in the car.

Because the clubhouse was quite a distance from the driving range, they were given a golf cart and Susan was content to sit and watch Hugh as he hit ball after ball with various clubs. After about twenty minutes she asked if she could try.

Hugh handed her his 3-wood, put a ball on a tee for her, showed her how to hold the club, and then stood back.

She lifted the club with a slow backswing and then came down with it as fast as she could. The ball went sailing off to the left, not at all where she wanted it to go. "Darn!" she exclaimed. "This is harder than it looks!"

Hugh knew that the problem was that she had raised her head and advised her to keep her head still. After a few more tries with the same result, he stood opposite her with his driver.

"Okay, Susan, here is what I am going to do to try to help you. I am going to rest the grip end of my driver on the top of your head when you take your stance and it will stay there while you swing so you will concentrate on keeping your head still. Don't worry about where the ball is going. Just watch your ball steadily as your club hits it off the tee. I'll watch the ball for you and, actually, you will have plenty of time to see your ball in the air after you complete your swing. Now keep your head still."

Hugh did exactly what he said he was going to do and the ball traveled perfectly straight toward the far flag she had been aiming at.

They repeated this about five more times and Susan smiled, "You are right, Hugh; this is a great way to relieve some stress."

Hugh smiled with the thought of possibly teaching her how to play so he could have another excuse to see her out of the office and said, "There you go. Your first golf lesson. Let me know if you want another one. But for now, we had better get back to the office."

They grabbed a couple of sandwiches to go in the clubhouse and headed back to the office. It was late in the afternoon when Susan and Hugh learned about the rental car. They discussed whether they should put out an APB on the car with the state police in Minnesota.

Hugh thought about it, "No, Let's not make ourselves look more foolish than we are. Besides, we really don't know if they are anything but tourists at this point. We should just wait and see where they turn the car in. That is a pretty clever way to give us the slip but I doubt that it was intentional. Didn't the agent say it was fairly common to take a car from Minneapolis to Duluth because it is only a two-hour drive?"

"Yes, that's true and if you were a tourist from France and wanted to see this country, it would be better to see it from a car," Susan agreed. Hugh nods and thinks about that for a minute or two, then says, "Let's get back to the problem of infiltrating the Boss's meetings."

 **CHAPTER FIFTEEN**

Bed and Breakfast

Francois, Henri, Ruth, and Eve took I35 north to state road 33 with Ruth driving and Eve riding in the front while Francois and Henri rode in the back admiring the lush, green countryside.

They soon found the small town of Cloquet with the unusual gas station. There was a plaque noting that it was built in 1958. It had a cantilevered copper canopy that extended over the gas pumps. Also, beneath the canopy glass-walled lounge area where patrons could wait while their cars were being serviced.

It was so far from what they had expected that they were unimpressed. It seemed that the original plan to have an open station with the gasoline lines coming out of the ceiling instead of the usual gas pumps did not meet the fire code so that whole idea had to be abandoned. However, the gas station itself was still in operation and they took the opportunity to top off the tank of their rental car before continuing their travels.

None of this disappointment affected Ruth's appetite because she commented, "I've been told that the most American thing you can eat is a cheeseburger." And immediately pulled into Gordy's Hi-Hat Drive-in.

While reading the menu, they became confused over the selection of "root beer" and got into a discussion about what the term "root beer" meant.

When the waitress arrived, she explained to them it is a soft drink and asked them where they are from. She was quite impressed when they told her they came all the way from France to see the unique gas station.

They enjoyed cheeseburgers, french fries, and root beer and discussed what they should do next.

Eve suggested they drive on into Duluth and find a nice place to spend the night. Ruth, knowing what she was thinking, shook her head slightly saying, "Yes, that sounds like a good idea." They talked about the fact that driving on the interstate highway is almost as bad as flying as far as seeing the country goes. Francois volunteered to drive for a while and Ruth handed him the key.

"I'll navigate," she said as she headed for the front passenger seat.

Turning to Eve and Henri, she chided, "Do you think you two could sit in the back and behave yourselves?"

"Why does she treat us like children?" they both say in unison like a pair of twins, staring at each other and trying not to laugh.

They tried to hide their sheepish grins as they climbed into the back seat. Henri turned his head away to look out their window but dropped one hand on the seat between them, open palm up. Eve glanced at his hand and put hers down on top of it, intertwining her fingers with his while giving him a little squeeze. Henri glanced at her and winked. They both sat back comfortably and rode on happily.

As soon as Francois and Ruth got in the front seats. Ruth reached into the glove compartment to pull out a map. She unfolded it in her lap and studied it for a moment looking for a back road to Duluth.

Finally, she pointed through the side window and said to Francois, "Just turn right at that corner onto

North Cloquet Road and we should have a nice quiet drive through the countryside back to I35 towards Duluth. It will also save gas if you keep it down to around 40 miles per hour."

Francois drove as instructed. Sure enough, it was a nice quiet road. They all relaxed and talked about how disappointed they were at the unusual gas station. They conclude that the other places they need to visit should be much better. Feeling a little defensive about this small disappointment, Ruth explained that their father wanted them to become familiar with the work of Frank Lloyd Wright in order to help in his company's mission in America which is to design a combination of churches, synagogues, and mosques for a College of Religions. His company got the job because of his reputation and the land had already been purchased for it near Las Vegas, Nevada. That's why they are there. Their father's other instruction was to become familiar with the U.S.A. because they may need to be there for quite a while.

As they drove along, Eve, still worried about her possible relationship with Henri was trying to cool things by studying the ads for hotels in Duluth from the brochures that she picked up.

"Here's one, Cotton Mansion. It caters to newlyweds, particularly those who elope. But the rooms are $309 per night."

"Forget that," said Ruth, realizing it was the same place she mentioned on the airplane, "Find something else."

"Maybe you'll like this one better; The Inn, overlooking Lake Superior at $120 per night."

"That's more like it. Give me the address and we'll put it in the GPS here."

She does so just as they enter I35 and head toward Duluth.

It was a long day. Everyone was tired. They checked into two separate rooms at The Inn, had dinner together, and sat down to enjoy the view of Lake Superior and plan for tomorrow. It is a beautiful view and they all commented on how pretty the lake is at this time of the evening.

"It is like looking at a peaceful ocean," Eve commented.

"Yes, the lake is so big that you cannot see the opposite shoreline," Henri agreed.

"I wonder why the shoreline is full of dark, rocky boulders instead of sand?" Ruth asked.

"Look, there is a horse and carriage coming up to the Inn. If I can arrange a ride in it, Ruth, would you like to go?" Francois asks.

Ruth smiled and assented, so Francois dashed into the room to call down to the concierge.

Realizing that they would be left alone again, Eve announced that she was going to take advantage of the indoor swimming pool and possibly the sauna before bed and walked off the balcony to change.

Henri now left alone, decided it was probably for the better until they could discover whether he and Eve were actually related. Propping his feet up on the balcony railing, he leaned his head back, closed his eyes, and simply enjoyed the feel of the breeze blowing off the lake. He is glad to be out of Algiers and glad to be away from the constant nagging of the Boss. Once the sun went down, he felt a little chilly and went inside.

The next destination would be the Robie House at the University of Chicago. Henri wondered how he and Francois might manage to land a pair of language teaching jobs at some university in the United States.

Once the others returned, Henri brought a bottle of wine into the girl's room so they could look at the map again and see if he could talk them into staying off the main road. After two glasses of wine each, they decided to avoid I94 and take the scenic route which went through Clinton, Iowa, even though it would take more than 12 hours to drive. They all agreed they were in no hurry and decided it was late so Francois and Henri headed back to their rooms.

As Ruth and Eve climbed into bed, Ruth said, "In reading about Chicago, I found that both the home and studio of Frank Lloyd Wright were near Chicago in Oak Park, Illinois. I wonder why Dad didn't add that to the places we should visit."

"Maybe he was testing us to see if we were smart enough to find it."

"You might be right. I know what I will do. We'll stop there and I'll call him and say 'Guess where we are?' That should be a nice surprise. Do you think I should tell him about Francois and Henri?"

Eve took a deep breath, let it out slowly, and turned to Ruth, "You had better break it to him slowly that they are on this trip with us. He might not think it is such a great idea."

"Don't worry," Ruth replied. "He knows we are big girls and can take care of ourselves."

The next morning, they rose early, checked out, and hit the road with Francois driving.

Francois suggested they might enjoy Eagle Point Park just before they get to Clinton, Iowa.

Francois said he had read somewhere that Eagle Point Park overlooked the widest part of the Mississippi River and he was anxious to see the view. When they got there, they found it was a very big park with lots of walking. One of the main features was a round stone castle turret with steps to the top around the inner edge and a series of windows to look out while you climbed the steps.

When they reached the top, the view was spectacular but Ruth kept looking back at the design and construction of the turret. Eve noticed how enthralled Ruth seemed and said, "What are you studying so hard?"

"You know, there is a lot of interesting architecture besides Frank Lloyd Wright's. I can see some interesting possibilities here by modernizing this turret design with that of the very first building we saw of Wright's in New York. I'll have to think about it."

Turning to Francois, Ruth went on to say, "Thank you for bringing us here. It's been very enlightening."

While driving around Clinton they passed the Fisher House.

Eve said, "Stop a minute, Francois; I want to ask you something."

Francois pulled over to the curb and as soon as he stopped, Eve said, "We just passed a beautiful home that had a sign out front that said, Bed and Breakfast." Does that mean the people who live there are renting out some of their rooms to tourists like us?"

"Yes, that is exactly what it means. I read about it in a tourist guidebook I found at the airport in Paris before we left. It said that if you would like to meet some Americans while you are there, one good way to do that is to stop at a home that advertises Bed and Breakfast instead of going to a hotel. It went on to say that another advantage of doing that is an opportunity to meet other tourists like yourself. If you also want to do that, be sure to pick one that has several rooms and a large dining table where all the guests gather for breakfast."

"That sounds like just what we should do. After all, to learn about the country, we need to do much more than going sightseeing. We need to meet the people. Let's turn around and go back. That was a beautiful home we passed with the Bed and Breakfast sign. This could be a good plan for our whole trip."

They all agreed and were in happy anticipation when they approached the Fisher House.

They had to explain that they were tourists from France, not two couples, and would need two rooms, one for the men and one for the ladies. They were told that the place was all booked up except for one very large room with two king-sized beds if they would like to "make do."

The four of them raised their eyebrows and looked at each other while a chorus of "That's fine with me," arose in French.

While checking in, Henri remarked that he needed to do a little shopping and asked if there were any men's clothing stores nearby.

The clerk pointed and said, "If you go down the street two blocks that way and turn right one block you will find a big shopping mall on the next corner. I am sure you can find whatever you want to buy there."

Henri turned to walk out the door when Eve said, "Wait, I'll go with you. I need the exercise."

They walked out, hand in hand, like a couple of teenagers.

As they walked along, Eve asked, "What do you need to buy?"

"Pajamas."

"You mean you didn't bring any pajamas?" she teased.

"No, I usually just sleep in my shorts. But I think I need pajamas for tonight."

"Yes, I think you are right. I'll bet you would look good in some blue pajamas."

They continued walking through the mall they had entered and soon found a nice-looking men's clothing store and went in.

Eve picked up a blue pair and asked, "How about these?"

"That's fine if you like them."

Eve handed them to the clerk and asked, "Do you also have these in pink?"

"No, but we have them in red or green."

"Red is close enough. Let's get two pairs. I need some too. I only brought a thin gown that you can probably see through."

Henri, "Oh, my. Maybe this trip to the store wasn't as good an idea as I thought."

Eve laughed, "Later, honey, later."

They returned, carrying their packages, smiling and laughing all the way.

Once back at the Fisher House, Ruth and Francois were waiting. "Did you find what you were looking for?" Ruth asked.

They both smiled broadly and assured her that they had.

"Good," she says, "because Francois and I are starving. We also took a little walk and found a local diner that seems to have a decent menu for dinner and a great view."

"Put your things down and let's go," Francois chimed in. "The walk will do us good after being in the car for so long."

The four headed off to try typical American cuisine and after dinner decided to take a stroll along the river. They walked hand in hand, stopping to admire how wide the river was and how beautifully the flower-rimmed trees looked. It was a warm summer evening with a light cool breeze blowing off the water. Francois put his arm around Ruth's shoulders as they stood for a while taking in the view.

"This is a beautiful part of the country, so quiet, so peaceful, not at all like back home," he said to her.

"Yes," she agreed. "I don't really miss the hustle and bustle of Paris when I am here with you."

She looked up at him and he leaned down giving her a long, soft kiss, his lips gently caressing hers until the silence was broken.

"Get a room!" he heard Henri shout as he and Eve approached them.

"We have one!" Francois shouted back. "Perhaps it is time to walk back."

"Yes," Henri agreed. "Time to walk back and for you to take a cold shower before retiring. I don't want any hot and bothered brother sleeping next to me."

They laughed and headed back to the Fisher House.

The next morning, sitting around the table with all the other guests at breakfast, it was even more fun when they found that two of the other couples there had recently been to Paris on vacation and could speak a little French. These two couples were both married, lived in New York, and were on their way back home, driving together. The two ladies both worked as dancers in the group known as the Rockettes that danced at the Radio City Music Hall. This was all very fascinating to Ruth and Eve who told them it had always been their secret ambition to dance in the Rockettes at Radio City.

As they drove away, the conversation in the car was all about their pleasant experience.

"Did you notice how broad-minded those people were? No one asked if we were married," Francois said.

"We must have looked like a couple of married couples to them," Henri replied.

"We could probably learn more about America and meet more nice people by staying at Bed and Breakfast places instead of hotels," Ruth exclaimed.

"I think that's a good idea. Let's do that. After all, getting to know the country is more than seeing it. It's even more important to get to know the people." Eve added, enthusiastically.

 **CHAPTER SIXTEEN**

Ruth Calls Dad

It was only a short drive into Oak Park which is really just a section of Chicago and Ruth couldn't wait to call her dad. Because of the time difference, it was very early morning there and he was groggy when she woke him up.

"Guess where we are now," Ruth said excitedly when he answered the phone.

"I haven't the faintest," he replied, trying to sound awake as he rubbed his eyes and yawned.

"We're at Oak Park, the home of Frank Lloyd Wright."

"I knew you would find it if you thought of it. How is the trip going? Have you met anyone interesting?"

"That's what I want to tell you about. We had to come all the way to the U.S.A. to meet two wonderful Frenchmen, Francois and Henri. They were also making a trip to Las Vegas and we met them on the plane when we left New York."

Suddenly realizing by the sound of his daughter's voice that he needed to be more awake for this conversation, he headed for the kitchen to make coffee.

"You said 'wonderful.' What's wonderful about them?"

"Well, Francois is the only one that's wonderful, Dad; I think I'm falling in love with him. And Henri looks so much like Eve that it's scary. In fact, she has done her DNA thing and sent the samples off to be analyzed. Meantime she is trying to keep him at arm's length, but they also seem to have a strong attraction for each other."

"And what about you? Are you also keeping Francois at arm's length?" her father questioned.

"Oh, Dad, you know me. Hugs and kisses are free. It's the rest you have to fight for," Ruth and her father laughed.

He did know his daughters well and trusted them. But his fatherly protective instincts could not help but kick in with his daughters so far away.

"What do you know about these two supposedly wonderful men?" he asked.

"Well, they were both adopted out of an orphanage in Algiers. Isn't that a coincidence?" She went on before he could answer her, "They were both language professors and had so much vacation time, we brought them on this trip with us...."

"Are they with you now?" he asked before taking a large gulp of hot coffee and almost burning his mouth.

"Of course, Francois is right here," she said, smiling at Francois.

"Good, let me talk to him a minute," he said, trying not to sound too concerned.

"Hello, Mr. Cohen, this is Francois," Francois said.

There was a pause on the line, as much deliberately for effect as to allow himself another sip of coffee to think about how he was going to talk to this strange man his daughter thought she was in love with.

"Hello. I wanted to talk to you because normally, I meet my daughters' friends before they go out with them, but that is not possible in this situation. I taught my daughters to be open to all people and not distrust them until they prove distrustful. Ruth has let me know that you have both been acting as gentlemen so far on this trip."

"Yes, sir, we are mindful that they are a little younger than both of us, but we were both so drawn to them, that it was hard not to take them up on their invitation," he assured her father.

"That's good. I hope your intentions stay honorable as I wouldn't want my daughters to be hurt in any way. I am sure Ruth and Eve have told you something about me, but I want to make it clear to you that I have friends in high places in America, and if any harm should come to them, well, let's just say, you would not like the outcome," he said, a little sternly.

"Oh, don't worry, sir. In fact, I am beginning to care deeply for your daughter and wouldn't hurt a hair on her head," he assured him. "In fact, I think Henri feels the same way about Eve, although it may end up that they are related, even possibly brother and sister, so Henri is being extra respectful."

"That's what I wanted to hear," he replied. "Can you put Ruth back on the phone?"

Francois handed the phone to Ruth. Jacob did not detect anything but an honest comment from Francois, so he sat back in his chair somewhat at ease as he spoke to Ruth.

"It sounds like you are having a wonderful time. Just be careful. Vacation romances don't always end in marriage. I would feel better if you took things more slowly until you were absolutely sure of his intentions. Are you going to the Robie House today?"

"Yes, to both, dad. That's where we are headed now."

"Okay, keep in touch. Love you. Bye."

"Love you too, dad. Bye."

Jacob went to his home office to check the girls' itinerary to see when they would be back in Las Vegas and made a note to call them if he had not heard from them upon their return.

They visited both the Robie House and the Unity Temple. They took the guided tours in both places and were quite impressed with the architecture in both places, particularly the design of the stained-glass windows which admitted plenty of warm, filtered light. Ruth commented that the Unity Temple seemed like it could easily serve as a mosque or synagogue but looked too much like a fort to be a Christian church.

Francois suggested that the process of making three different buildings may be, not only overly ambitious but could be self-defeating. After all, persuading students to take a course in someone else's religion is going to be hard enough without expecting them to walk into a strange building.

Agreeing, Ruth replied, "Yes, nothing about this is going to be easy. Seeing the Unity Church is certainly inspiring enough to make us consider that a single building would be a better choice. The more I think about it, the more I agree with you, Francois. I really appreciate the interest you are taking in these problems. It means a lot to me."

 # CHAPTER SEVENTEEN

Hugh and Susan's Date

As Hugh climbed in his car and started towards Susan's condo to pick her up for dinner, he noticed a few sprinkles on the windshield.

"So, we'll have some rain tonight," he said to himself. "That's fine. It'll make for a cozier evening. I can't believe how lucky I am to have Susan helping me with this task."

He glanced at his watch as he pulled into her condo complex, right on time. As he pulled up, near her front door, she came running out with a newspaper over her head, snatched the car door open, and jumped in.

"Just trying to keep my hair dry," she says, "I don't mind the rain. It tends to make for a cozier evening."

Hugh broke out in a broad grin

"What are you laughing at? Did I say something funny?"

"No, I'm just smiling because that's exactly what I said to myself when I saw the drops on the windshield. What a comfort to know that we think so much alike."

"Oh, my goodness, are we already that close?"

"Who knows?" Hugh murmured under his breath as he headed towards the highway again.

Attempting to start up a conversation, he said, "This is a very convenient place for you. It's a pleasant drive from downtown Washington."

"Yes, that's why my father bought it. When the FBI transferred him from Charleston to Washington, it was shortly after the big super-highway called the Beltway was completed and the several Real Estate Agents that he contacted all took him to places being developed outside the Beltway. It must have been the rainy season because he remembered them all as being huge mud holes. Anyway, he decided he did not want to look forward to driving around the Beltway to and from work each day so, he told the Real Estate Agent that he wanted to go down the Mount Vernon Memorial Highway as far as needed for him to afford it. The agent took him down to see these townhouses being built in this area called Carter Farm Court which is only about a half-mile off the Mount Vernon Parkway via Collingwood Road and he was delighted. My mother gave it to me when she decided to move back to Charleston after my father passed away. I love it here." *Oops, there I go again,* she thought to herself, "She feels more at home there because that's where almost all her brothers and sisters live."

"I have always heard it's a very nice city, but I have never been there. Did you say almost all her brothers and sisters? How many does she have?" he asked.

"Eight still living," Susan replied. "Four of each and only two live in other states."

Hugh pondered this. He only had one sister but had enjoyed a large number of aunts and uncles as he was growing up. Waxing nostalgia made him uncomfortable so he changed the subject.

"I have worked up a pretty good appetite. Do you have a suggestion about where we should go to dinner?"

"My favorite place is nearby, in old town Alexandria. It's called Gadsby's Tavern."

"Oh, yes. It's one of my favorite places too. What a coincidence. I've heard it was one of George Washington's favorite hangouts," Hugh says, nervously. He felt a little anxious and was trying hard to please.

Hugh drove on slowly as they proceeded to Gadsby's Tavern. It is a nice, upscale restaurant with a fireplace in the main dining room. They found a quiet table next to a window where they could talk.

Looking out the window, they noticed it was now pouring down rain. They both smiled and said, "Cozy," at the same time.

Susan ordered a steak, medium rare with a baked potato and the house salad and Hugh said, "I'll have the same."

Susan, anxious to hear more about Hugh's ideas, prodded, "Now, tell me all about your plan for a College of Religions."

"Well, it's not much more than a dream, really. I may have mentioned before that I think civilization progresses in two ways, either by invention or by education. I have always thought that if religious people learned more about the religious beliefs of other people, they would be much more tolerant of them and religious wars would cease. You seem to have experienced that when you read the Koran. I am sure that if people of the three major religions, Christians, Jews, and Muslims studied it they would be impressed by the similarities. My plan would be to start by building a church, a synagogue and a mosque side by side and have students go to each one for instructions learning about all three thoroughly; then expand it to include other religions. What do you think?"

"I think that's probably true. I love it. After all, the Koran has more references to Moses than anyone else. I'll bet there are practically no Jewish people who know that. However, think of the obstacles. How would you ever get any students to sign up for that?"

"That's undoubtedly the major problem. You would probably have to find some way to make it compulsory, like putting it in one of the Service Academy's required curricula. Even then, there would be a lot of opposition."

"Anyway, I love the whole idea."

Just then the waiter came with their dinners. The steaks were cooked to perfection, with a little char on the outside and a reddish pink on the inside. As they dug in and took their first bites, they simultaneously moaned at the delicious tenderness of the meat melting in their mouths.

"I guess we both enjoy the taste of an excellent steak," Hugh said while Susan could only smile and nod her head in agreement as she cut another piece.

Hugh was relieved that Susan had a hearty appetite. Other women that he had dated would either eat only a few bites of the meal and then complain about it or order only a small appetizer both of which exasperated him to no end and would result in no further dates.

While they were driving home, Hugh asked, "You don't smoke, do you?"

"No, but smoke doesn't bother me. You go ahead if you want to."

Hugh sighed and said, "A cigar always tastes best after a good meal."

"I know. My dad used to say the same thing. I always loved the smell of a good cigar."

When they stopped at a traffic light, Hugh pulled out a cigar and lit it.

Susan, a little nervous about asking a personal question, said, "We have talked a lot about everything else. Will you tell me about yourself? Have you been married?"

"Yes, I am a widower with three teenage children," Hugh replied, reluctantly. "My wife had breast cancer which metastasized rapidly. It reached the frontal lobes of her brain and destroyed her personality."

Susan was stunned. She thought about that for a long time, trying to think of something to say.

Finally, she said, "That's terrible, how did she change?"

Hugh replied, "She seemed to think it was her duty to change the world. She started doing odd things that she would never think of doing before. For instance, once she snatched the cigarette out of someone's mouth and gave them a lecture on the evils of smoking. She had become hypercritical and had a hard time de-escalating once she got angry."

They drove on quietly through the rain as Susan processed this and felt a lot of sympathy for him.

"Well, I feel obligated to tell you something about myself," Susan said, "I know you think I am very young and inexperienced but I am not. I thought I was in love with a man and stayed with him for three months before I discovered he was dating two other girls at the same time."

Hugh had no reply to that. He just shook his head.

When they reached Susan's condo, she said, "Just stop near the front door and I'll run in."

She picked up the newspaper to hold over her head saying, "Thanks for a lovely evening but no kissing goodnight on the first date."

She yanked open the car door, closed it, looked back with a smile, and ran in.

Hugh sat there, stunned. *Wait a minute*, he thought to himself, *wasn't this our second date? Maybe she didn't count our first dinner out as a date.*

He drove slowly away, thinking to himself, *well, she did use the word date! That's the most encouraging thing I heard all evening!*

 **CHAPTER EIGHTEEN**

The President

Although the rain that night had cooled things down to a pleasant 63 degrees, the next morning the temperature shot back up to June's normal 80 degrees by 9 a.m. As he got out of his car, Hugh kept his coat off as he walked into his office and simply slung it over the nearest chair and turned to make coffee. Thoughts of Susan distracted him, so his first attempt at coffee was far too strong for his taste.

The second attempt was much better, and as he sat at his desk and began to enjoy it, his mind wandered again to Susan. He couldn't get her off his mind. He kept thinking about how much he would like to get to know her without offending her.

Would she become offended because, after all, he is, in a way, her boss, and inter-office relationships are frowned upon? He would have to find a way around this problem somehow.

Shaking his head to try to clear it and re-focus on the day he reminded himself that he ought to concentrate on what he needed to say to the President. It is 9 a.m. and his meeting with the President is scheduled for 10. He pulled out a pad and started making some notes to himself when the phone rang.

"Hello."

The security guard was on the other end of the line.

"Mr. Montague, I hope you are expecting the President because he is on his way up to see you."

"The President? You mean he is here? I can't believe it. It is only 9:30. Are you sure he is here to see me?"

Just then the door opened and in walked the President. Hugh jumped to his feet.

"Sit down, sit down," the President said, grinning and motioning for Hugh to sit. "I just thought I would drop by to see how you are doing since my earlier meeting was so short. I don't want a formal, highly classified report. Just bring me up to speed on your progress."

"Yes sir, as you wish."

Hugh proceeded to tell him all about Susan's interview with the shoe-bomber, how he was foiled, and what little he knew about a man called "Boss." He described Tom's assumptions about a remote meeting place and Francois and Henri's attempt to buy mules, followed by their plan to lease them and ship them to Algiers. He further described the CIA's use of Deep Cover and how he intended to get messages transmitted by postcard. He further described how Tom and an FBI agent are now at the Grand Canyon prepping the two mules and that some of the postcards had already been written. He stressed what a big help Susan had been.

After listening intently, the President said, "I was sure that when I picked you for the job you would come up with a scheme that no one else would even think of and you have not disappointed me. I do have one small suggestion, though. The first time this becomes successful, "Boss," as you call him, will become suspicious and may think the mules are wired. You need to have a Plan B for that possible eventuality."

"You are absolutely right and we will have to talk about that the next time I report."

The President got up, smiled, and said, "Good job, keep it up," as he waved his right hand and left.

Hugh had started to rise but the President was gone too quickly. He plopped back down in his chair with a big sigh of relief and started to think about Susan again. "How could such a pretty girl be so smart?"

 # CHAPTER NINETEEN

Inter-faith Marriage

Ruth and Eve woke to a brisk sixty-degree morning. When Eve opened the sliding glass door to their balcony the wind from lake Michigan swept in and she shivered, quickly closing it again. Ruth snuggled under the covers.

"I think we need to purchase some heavier clothing before we leave," Eve suggested.

Ruth agreed from deep under the covers and told Eve she would make coffee for them if Eve would go down and pick out a couple of things for both of them to wear.

As Eve opened the door to her room, she saw Francois also leaving the door to his room.

"Where are you going?" she asked.

"Down to the lobby gift shop, I didn't realize it was so cold in Michigan until last night when Ruth and I took that carriage ride and by the time we got back it was too late to buy anything," he replied.

Eve nodded her head in agreement and said, "I am going that way also. I don't think Ruth and I realized that the United States was so vast that it could have drastically different climates between north and south. Silly, the things you just don't think about. Are you also shopping for Henri?"

"No," Francois replied. "He realized it last night when the temperature dropped as he was sitting on the balcony so he got to the gift shop before it closed. He told me that we could also expect Wisconsin to be no warmer than 73 degrees this time of year. Henri is always googling information so I guess he is usually more prepared than me."

Eve found gym outfits made of sweatshirt material and sporting an outline of Michigan on the front of the hoodies. She picked a blue set for Ruth and a pink set for herself.

Francois found a windbreaker type of jacket with UM emblazoned on the right breast and decided that would do.

After everyone gathered together and finished a pancake breakfast, they started the next leg of their trip with Francois driving and Ruth navigating. Eve and Henri rode in the back. Ruth pointed out that their next stop would be Racine, Wisconsin which was only a few miles up the road, and if they took route 41 it should be a pretty drive along the western edge of Lake Michigan. They needed to find a nice place where they could stay at least a couple of days because, in addition to the Johnson Way Building they wanted to see, the Frank Lloyd Wright Library which is also there.

There are quite a few small towns along the lake on route 41 and it should be easy to find a nice Bed and Breakfast which is what they were now looking for. Ruth informed everyone that there was one called Mansard's on The Lake which has kitchenettes in case any of them would like to try their hand at cooking.

A couple of groans came from the back seat so she said, "Okay, cancel that idea."

They continued up the road enjoying the beautiful scenery. They marveled at the height of the Ash and Aspen trees which Eve commented must be more than 80 feet tall. Francois and Henri were in awe at how lush the Maple trees were and when they passed a stand of White Cedars Eve took a deep breath and asked if everyone could smell the wonderful cedar smell that she was experiencing.

Henri googled information about the two states and found that bear, deer, cougar, and elk were common to the area, but strain as they might look out the windows, they could not see any wild animals.

Finally, they turned into downtown Racine where they came across a nice-looking home called Christmas House which advertised itself as a Bed and Breakfast.

After Francois pulled in and stopped, they all piled out to look around. Across the street from the house, they saw a huge park while further down past the end of the street was the lake. The three-story house itself is quite elegant and made more so by the two large flowering trees in the front yard.

"Look at those beautiful trees!" exclaimed Francois. "What kind are they?"

"I think they are called Japanese Cherry trees. They sure are pretty, aren't they?" volunteered Eve.

"Everything here seems so inviting. I'll bet this is a popular spot to visit all summer," said Henri.

Ruth volunteered to go in to inquire about a large room only to find that the best she could get was two connecting rooms for two nights. After talking it over, they decided it was such a nice place that they would take it. They all looked forward to meeting the other people who would be staying there.

Ruth was quicker than Eve at unpacking and wandered downstairs to the Christmas House library. She admired the beautiful cherry wood that enveloped the room which held tidy bookshelves that lined three walls and the comfortable, overstuffed chairs which snuggled into each corner with a reading lamp on each side table.

The owner of the Inn came in to see if she could help Ruth find a nice book, but Ruth told her she was more interested in the architecture and history of the house. As she looked out the large windows, past the front porch, she asked where all the people walking by could be going.

"It's the 4th of July. They are going to one of the largest 4th of July parades in the mid-west."

Ruth's eyes widened, "A parade! I love parades!" she squealed.

She found out when it started and the best place to watch it from and raced upstairs to tell the others.

"Oh, I completely forgot it was July 4th," Henri exclaimed. "That's America's birthday when they celebrate their independence from Great Britain. What a great opportunity to see how it is done."

They all agreed and quickly changed into fresh clothes with comfortable shoes and headed for the viewing spot that Ruth had been told about.

Crowds of people were lining the streets with vendors walking up and down selling everything from cotton candy to shaved ice. Henri bought each of them a cone of shaved ice just as the parade started to come by.

There were police officers on motorcycles leading the parade followed by a number of convertible cars with their tops down carrying various parade dignitaries.

They marveled at all the elaborate floats and marching bands. There seemed to be no end to them. The crowd clapped and cheered enthusiastically for each one as it passed by. Ruth, Francois, Eve, and Henri got caught up in the enthusiasm and found themselves cheering and clapping as much as anyone.

They laughed at the clowns and jugglers who seemed to pop up into the street out of nowhere. Francois paid one of the clowns to make Ruth a large, colorful balloon flower which he presented on bended knee to her delight.

Eve was taken by the beautiful, black Andalusian horses that pranced down the parade route in traditional Spanish garb.

There were more marching bands, more elaborate floats, and a vast array of people marching under banners of various charity groups. The Shriners had a drum and bugle corps and a clown car that stopped right in front of them. They all laughed as many more clowns than could possibly fit in the little car clambered out of it. They darted among the crowd giving candy to all the kids before folding themselves back into it and driving on.

It was certainly a wonderful spectacle for the four young foreigners. They were full of joy from being caught up in the entertainment of the parade. Henri tried his hand at juggling when a Mime came by and silently persuaded him to throw three balls in the air. They all laughed at his first three failed attempts but with a determined look on his face, he was successful until they all applauded and laughed so much that he lost his concentration. The Mime knew he was about to drop the balls so, as quick as a magician, his hands swiftly took the place of Henri's and recovered control of the juggling balls. As he walked away, he gave a wink and a nod to Henri.

"How did he do that?" Eve squealed in astonishment.

When the parade finished passing by them, Henri grabbed Eve in a big bear hug and said, "Come on, let's find some good place to have dinner. I'm starving."

It wasn't long before they came across a place called the Olde Madrid Restaurant. It had a menu printed and displayed outside for passers-by to peruse before coming in.

"This looks like a great place," Ruth said, "We can order some tapas to share, and then they have various paella dishes that also feeds three to four. Let's go in."

They ordered Carne empanadas, duck croquettes, and grilled veggie salad as their tapas and then settled for seafood paella. They tried the Spanish wine recommended by the waitress and had a wonderful time sitting outside in the cool summer air watching people as they ate.

To the group's amusement, Henri made up stories about the people as they passed by and they quickly all joined in taking turns guessing about someone's occupation and lifestyle. It was all in good fun and nothing derogatory was said.

The summer sun was slow to go down so it wasn't until ten o'clock that they made their way back to the Christmas House.

Ruth and Francois decided to sit in the rocking chairs on the porch for a while. Eve was exhausted so Henri walked her to her room. They stood by the door for a short while talking about what a wonderful time they had seeing the parade. Eve yawned and leaned against the door, "I'm sorry that I'm so tired but I really just want to go to bed," she said, sleepily.

"No need to apologize," Henri replied, as he squeezed her hand. "I would like to beat Francois to the shower, anyway. Goodnight," he said as he kissed her gently on the cheek.

Ruth and Francois were slowly rocking on the porch gazing out towards the street now silent and void of any street traffic. Ruth was thinking out loud, "You know, I really like the way American townhomes all seem to be on good size lots. There's so much room here. This is so different from Paris where, unless you are wealthy, townhomes are usually only a few feet apart if they are detached from their neighbor, and very few have more than just a patch of ground to grow a few flowers or vegetables."

Francois agreed and wondered if there was any way he could avoid going back to Algiers.

He said, "Ruth, I am so glad you invited us to come along on this trip. This country amazes me at every turn. There's so much freedom. And you are such an amazingly wonderful woman."

He got up from his rocking chair, held his hand out to her as she did likewise, and drew her into his arms. He looked steadily into her eyes as he kissed her and felt her return his passion.

"Is it too soon to tell you that I love you?" he whispered as their lips parted.

She smiled and kissed him again sweetly, gently, longingly.

"I love you too," she replied.

The next morning at breakfast, they met another couple from France and got into a long discussion about religion.

Francois pointed out that he and Henri were orphans brought up by a Muslim family although they had been in a Catholic orphanage for the first five years of their life. As young boys, the difference between Muslim and Catholic was very confusing and caused them to go through the motions to honor their adopted parents but to stop the practice when they grew into manhood.

The other couple told them about their family. The man was an Episcopalian and the former wife was a Catholic but it was the wife who, after having three children, insisted on a divorce. This, initially, confused the man because back in those early days divorce was unheard of in the Catholic tenets. He pointed out that even though the children were raised Catholic, only one child remained Catholic, one became a Lutheran, and one a Methodist. In the USA, all religions are equally acceptable.

Henri pointed out that even though the names of those religions were different, they were all Christ-based religions. His confusion came from the fact that Islam was not a Christ-based religion but prayed to the same God, the God of both Abraham and Isaac, and even recognized Christ's activities and teaching on earth and identified him as a prophet. He said that it seemed to him there were more similarities in the core values of those two religions than differences so the rift between them was hard to justify.

The husband added to the conversation that the daughter, who became a Methodist, met a man who had moved to the United States on a student visa from Iran. He was a Muslim and they were very much in love. However, the relationship ended when he wanted her to move to California with him as his second wife once he returned from his trip back to Iran to marry the woman his parents had picked out for him. So, it wasn't their religious differences that caused them to part ways, but the differences in what was socially acceptable. While in America, bigamy is a crime, in Iran, a man can have as many wives as he can afford.

Henri chimed in at this point, "Regardless of that law against bigamy, I still think there is much more freedom in this country than anywhere else I ever heard of. The more I learn about things here, the more I want to stay here. I wish we could find a way to do that. Do you think there is any demand for a pair of language professors?"

"I am sure that if you look in the right place you could find that," the man said, encouragingly.

Ruth, Eve, Francois and Henri spent two days and nights in Racine dutifully visiting all of Frank Lloyd Wright's buildings and taking related tours without finding anything they could count as helpful toward their designing either a church, a synagogue, or a mosque.

The more they talked about the Unity Church they had previously seen and liked, the more they concluded that a single building of a neutral design would be much more practical for their purposes.

It fell upon Ruth the responsibility to explain that to her father and sell him on the idea.

While they slept separately in adjoining rooms, they became closer and closer together with their pajama parties. They drank a little wine, played cards and mostly watched television. Francois was especially interested in, what seemed quaint expressions in English that he had never heard before and said that it helped him learn more of the language.

Ruth was impressed with how gentlemanly the men were while Eve was still deeply concerned about the question of whether or not she and Henri might turn out to be closely related.

At breakfast the next morning, Ruth pointed out that the next leg of their trip would be a long one, Racine to Pittsburg was over 500 miles, and if they want to see some of the country in between they ought to make one or two stops.

"My map shows we will have to go back through Chicago, then across two states, Indiana and Ohio plus a large part of Pennsylvania to get to Pittsburg. Also, Falling Waters is not really in Pittsburg but over 60 miles to the southeast in a little town called Mill Run.

She explained that her father had expected them to fly to these various places and rent a car to get there so he had listed the city nearby with an airport. They all agreed that they were in no hurry and reminded her they wanted to continue to meet more Americans along the way. They decided to head south on the pretty road along the lake and try to avoid big interstate highways on the trip.

As they drove along, Ruth was sitting closer to Francois and sometimes holding his right hand while he drove with his left. She was quietly thinking for a long time. She looked in the back seat and found that Henri and Eve had fallen asleep. Finally, she turned to Francois and whispered, "Are you really thinking about staying in America?"

"It's a lot more than that, Ruth. I am definitely falling in love with you and Henri has told me he is in love with Eve and we know we cannot take you back to Algiers so there seems to be no other choice. In addition, we love the amount of freedom here in America. How long do you two expect to be here?"

"Oh, Francois, you take my breath away!"

He turned to give her a long, loving look, but unwillingly also turned the wheel to the right.

"Watch out! Keep your eyes on the road!

He quickly corrected his driving with no harm done.

Ruth let out a sigh of relief and continued, "We may be here indefinitely. My dad is setting up a branch office in Las Vegas for developing the buildings for a college in Nevada. I don't know how long he expects us to stay and work for him here but we have no big incentive to go back to France other than being a little home-sick."

"The next time you write or talk to him, be sure to thank him for this trip he instructed you to make."

"I have an idea. You initially said your time was limited to two weeks. We only have one more place to visit, a place called Falling Waters near Mill Run, Pennsylvania and we still have a few days left before we have to fly back to Las Vegas from Pittsburgh so why don't we visit a few colleges along the way as we cross Indiana and Ohio? That way, you could inquire about their foreign language departments and see if you could fit in somewhere."

"That sounds like a good idea. Sometimes I think you are full of good ideas. Does your map show any candidate colleges along the way that we should consider?"

Ruth pulled out her map and started to study it.

"Here's a good place to start. South Bend, Indiana, where the University of Notre Dame, is located. I've heard about it and always wanted to visit it."

They started south on the now familiar and scenic route 42. When he saw the signs indicating the University of Chicago, he turned off the highway to drive through the campus just to see what it looked like. They were not going to stop because they had already decided they had no interest in living in Chicago. Driving through the campus, they were somewhat surprised at the depressingly Gothic architecture, several of the buildings virtually covered with ivy and many large trees keeping everything relatively dark.

Disappointed, they returned to route 42 and continued around the lake until they picked up route 20 towards South Bend and Notre Dame.

 # CHAPTER TWENTY

Plan B

Susan had just gotten to Hugh's office and settled into one of the comfortable chairs with her morning cup of coffee when Tom unexpectedly walked in.

"You're back already. That was a quick trip," she said as Hugh looked up from his desk, also apparently surprised.

"Yes, I found that I didn't have to drive from Las Vegas to Tusayan, Arizona where the mules are because there is a small airport there. I met the two mules, a male and a female, got to know them and gained their confidence. By the way, they have names. Their names are..."

"Stop right there, interrupts Hugh, don't tell me their names. Susan and I have re-christened them. From now on they will be known as 'Ward' and 'Heather.'"

"Okay, that's fine," said Tom, shrugging his shoulders. "That must mean you have started writing the postcards."

"Correct."

Tom seemed to be a little tired. He walked over to the other easy chair opposite Susan and plopped down in it with a sigh.

"How did the meeting with the President go?" Tom inquired.

"Fine. He had one good suggestion which we probably would have thought of in time. He said when we become successful, the Boss will become suspicious and may think that the mules are wired. He wants us to have a Plan B to implement at that time. I told him we would have that in time for our next report which means you need to work something out with your vets and let me know what it is."

"Good, no problem. We'll work something out. I only got the mules prepared; I will wait until they are in Algiers where we will install the listening devices. That way, our vets there will be taking over full responsibility. They will like everything much better that way."

"That's a very good point, Tom. I knew you could handle it. Tell me about the mules."

"They are very docile and quite valuable to those who own them. That's why, when those two Frenchmen tried to buy them, they couldn't. They could only lease two for a period of three months and had to wait three weeks before they could be shipped to Algiers. So, we have some time to get things prepared."

"Good, you can take our postcards and mail one back from London to Jane for our initial test then contact your vets and other CIA agents to get everything set up. Also, come back with a Plan B. I can't believe we didn't see the need for that before the President did."

Tom rose to leave, "Yes, you are right. We should have thought of that. Well, goodbye and good luck." He picked up the postcards and left.

 # CHAPTER TWENTY-ONE

Jane

Jane and her husband, Henry, lived in a nice suburban home in the outskirts of Winston Salem, North Carolina. It was a hot, muggy July morning which was about to spoil her mood. As usual, she walked down her driveway, opened her mailbox and gathered up her mail. "Bills, bills, bills," she muttered as she thumbed through the envelopes. Suddenly, bewildered, she saw a postcard from London.

"What's this?" she says, as she turns the postcard over and notices it is from London. "Having a wonderful time. Wish you were here" signed, "Your favorite mule, Ward."

She said to herself, "This has got to be one of Kate's jokes! She never told me she was going to London. Maybe she is back. I'll give her a call."

As soon as she got back in the house, she put down the rest of the mail, picked up the phone and dialed Kate's number.

"Hello, Jane?" Kate said, delighted to hear from her old friend.

"Kate, you never told me you were going to London. When did you get back?"

"What are you talking about? I haven't been to London."

"I just got this postcard from London and it must be one of your jokes. It says, 'Having a wonderful time, wish you were here.' And it's signed, 'Your favorite mule, Ward.' Who else could have written it?"

Kate laughed. "Someone must be playing a joke on you. After all these years, who do you know in London that knows about those two mules we rode down into the Grand Canyon?"

"I have no idea. I told a lot of people about that after we graduated from college but who would remember after all these years? Besides, I have moved several times since then. Who, other than you, would know my address?"

"I can't imagine who it would be. Maybe Jim knows. I'll ask him when he gets home. Wait, here he comes now." Kate put the receiver down and stood to give her husband a hug when he came in.

"Hi, honey. Who are you talking to?" Jim asked as he kissed her on the cheek.

"It's Jane. She's gotten a postcard from London signed, 'Your favorite mule, Ward.' You remember I told you about us riding the mules, Ward and Heather, down into the Grand Canyon. Who do you know in London?"

"I don't know anyone in London and I certainly don't know any mules that can write. It's just someone's joke. Maybe you'll get one from Heather. Tell her to save it. Maybe we can recognize the handwriting."

Back into the phone, Kate says, "Did you hear all of that?"

"Yes, I'll save it."

 # CHAPTER TWENTY-TWO

Notre Dame

Francois, Henri, Ruth, and Eve arrived in South Bend, Indiana about mid-day and decided to park the car and stretch their legs.

Eve spotted the Circa Art Gallery and coaxed them all in for a look around. Eve and Ruth were surprised at the reasonable prices of many of the original pieces hanging in the gallery and made a mental note of those they liked that may be appropriate for the building Ruth was tasked to design.

As they left, Francois and Henri stopped to read a poster advertising the East Race Waterway.

"Are you girls up for a little excitement?" Francois asked.

Eve and Ruth joined them at the poster and agreed that it looked like great fun for the afternoon. Francois made a note of the address and they found the launch area without difficulty.

There were many blue rubber boats sitting on the banks. Some of them were only big enough for two people. There was a medium size one that appeared to hold five or six people and larger ones that could hold eight or ten. The smaller ones were actually kayaks. Although Henri and Francois thought those were a good idea because Henri and Eve could go in one while Francois and Ruth followed in another, the girls put an end to that. Neither of them was versed in the art of canoeing and were unsure about Francois and Henri, so they put their foot down and stressed that they wanted to all be together in one boat.

"Do you know how to do this?" Ruth asked in order to confirm her suspicions.

"Sure," Francois replied. "The large flat part goes in the water and you hang on to the smaller end to steer. How hard could it be?" he continued with a shrug of the shoulders.

Ruth raised her eyebrows looking doubtful and looked at Eve who turned to their outfitter and asked, "Is this safe for beginners?"

The outfitter looked at the four of them and smiled. "Almost all of our customers are beginners. I will explain everything to you before you get into the raft," he replied calmly, as he chose a medium size raft for them.

Ruth and Eve took a deep breath and made sure they listened intently to the outfitter as he instructed them how to handle the boat in the white water.

"Got it!" said Francois and Henri in unison. The girls climbed in first, followed by Henri and, finally by Francois.

The outfitter shoved them off, telling them that another person would meet them at the end of the run.

All was going well and they excitedly maneuvered through the first set of white-water current. Francois was the rudder man at the stern, Henri was in the bow and the girls were in the middle. Eve was leaning over the side, running her hand in the water when suddenly they hit a bump and she tumbled into the water.

Francois yelled to get Henri and Ruth to backstroke with their paddles while he reached his long oar out to Eve who was swimming towards them. She grabbed the end of the oar and Francois pulled her back and into the boat.

As they were talking about what had happened, they had not noticed that they were fast approaching another, longer section of white water. The raft began to toss and everyone scrambled to their oars. Henri yelled to the girls to put down their oars and just hold on which they obediently and gladly did while both men maneuvered the raft, up, down then sideways the raft bounced as Francois and Henri, working together managed to get the raft safely through the rapids.

Once on the other side, they saw the landing with a young man waving to them to maneuver the boat towards him.

"Is everyone okay?" he asked, nervously when he saw that Eve was completely soaked. He helped her out of the raft first, then gave her a large towel that wrapped all around her from shoulder to knees.

"Yes," Henri replied as he attempted to help Eve dry off. He picked up a smaller towel for her hair. "We just lost our minds for a second or two, but it's okay, now."

Francois and Ruth told him that it was great fun and thanked him for the towels.

"It's a nice sunny day if you want to walk back along the river path to your car. It's about a two-mile walk. Otherwise, a tram will be along in a few minutes to give you a ride."

"Let's walk," Eve said. "It will give my clothes a chance to dry off."

"When you get back, there's a bin to drop the towels in," he said as he waved goodbye to them.

They strolled along, enjoying the view, and noticed that every fifty yards or so, there was a park bench. About a mile down, they found a bench in a small bit of shade near a sun-drenched grassy spot where Eve could lay out her towel and enjoy some sunbathing to help her clothes dry out.

Ruth and Francois decided to check their cell phones to look for a Bed and Breakfast. They found a quaint one called "Innisfree," which was across the river from the University of Notre Dame. When Ruth called, she found out the only room available was the top floor room, which would accommodate all four of them. She relayed the information to Francois.

"That is very tempting, but I am afraid I am too attracted to you to behave if we sleep in the same room together," he said with a smile and a wink.

Ruth blushed and smiled back. "Okay, I will look further."

They settled for a Hilton Inn and Suites, which offered free breakfast, free Wi-Fi, an exercise room, and a swimming pool. "I don't know if Eve is up for swimming again," Ruth teased, "but I wouldn't mind enjoying the pool later."

Once at the Hilton, they learned that not far away was Four Winds Field which was holding a baseball game at 5:00. Seeing American baseball live would be a real treat for Francois and Henri. They didn't care who was playing; they would just applaud the good plays. Ruth and Eve joined in their enthusiasm and got caught up in the game as well. Throughout the game, they called out to the people hawking peanuts and beer, thoroughly enjoying the experience.

When the fifth inning started, Ruth and Eve excused themselves to use the powder room and came back with hamburgers, hot dogs, and more beer. Everyone was just a little drunk when they got back to the Hilton. Ruth declared that she was going for an evening swim. Eve opted for a soak in a hot bath and then settled in to watch a movie when a knock came at the door.

"Francois went down for a swim with Ruth, so I thought I might see what you are up to," Henri said as he stood at the door.

"Come on in. I was just about to relax and watch a movie on TV," Eve replied.

She sat on the edge of the bed flipping through the movies available on TV until they found one that they both agreed on. Eve crawled up to the head of the bed. Henri was sitting in a chair, but Eve could tell that he seemed uncomfortable.

"Do you want to come up and relax on the bed beside me?" she asked, somewhat hesitantly.

"If you are sure that's okay," he replied and slowly got up and slid onto the bed beside her.

Needless to say, it was hard for them to concentrate on the movie. Eve kept switching positions on the bed, from leaning back against the headboard to sitting upright with her knees tucked up against her chest. Henri kept switching from laying on his stomach trying to watch, to sitting up, relaxing and leaning against the headboard.

Halfway through the movie, Henri jumped up and exclaimed, "I can't do this! You are too enticing! I wish I hadn't taken that DNA test to see if you were my sister! I have to go!" and he left the room without a response from Eve.

When Ruth got to the pool, there was no one else around. She slipped into the water and began to swim laps. It was relaxing to feel the cool water against her as she glided effortlessly through it. All was silent, and the exercise was beginning to sober her up. After about four laps, Francois appeared beside her, and they swam another lap together.

When they got back to the shallow end, Francois leaned against the side of the pool, and Ruth swam into his arms. No words needed to be said. He moved away from the side of the pool and held her in his arms. He moved them about the pool as if in a dance, all the while showering each other with kisses. She wrapped her legs around his waist and kissed him with an urgency that let him know he was loved and wanted. Then, they heard someone coughing.

"I hate to break this up, but the pool closes at midnight."

Francois and Ruth turned their heads in unison towards the sound of the voice and saw the night watchman standing at the edge of the pool.

"You do have a room here, don't you?" he asked.

"Oh, yes, sir," they replied, again in unison.

"I suggest you head that way," he replied.

They quickly got out of the pool, grabbed their towels and room keys, and headed for the elevator.

"Perhaps if you would come to my room, I could persuade Henri to leave us alone for a while so we could continue what we started at the pool," Francois said as he reached for Ruth.

Before she could answer, the elevator door opened to their floor, and they walked out. Just as Francois was putting his key card in the door, they saw Henri striding down the hall as if on a mission. He did not look happy. When he saw them, he just growled and pushed open the door.

Francois turned to Ruth and said, "Well, perhaps not tonight. I had better see what he is so mad about."

He gave her a quick kiss and went inside.

Henri's action caused Ruth to be concerned for her sister, so she quickly went back to her room.

She found Eve lying on the bed sobbing.

"I've ruined everything!" she blubbered between tears, "Henri hates me now! Why did I ever have to insist on that DNA test?" she looked at Ruth with red, tear-stained eyes.

"Did he hurt you?" Ruth asked hesitantly.

"Only my heart!" she cried, and between the sobs, she told Ruth what had happened.

Ruth sat next to her, rubbing her back to comfort her, and in the most sympathetic way she could, she said, "Dear Eve, sometimes I don't think you know just how beautiful you are and the effect you have on men. It is so obvious that Henri is besotted with you, and, apparently being so close to you and alone with you in a hotel room was just too hard for him to control his desire for you."

Giving her a hug, she continued, "Sweetie, he doesn't hate you. He loves you and not in a brotherly sort of way."

Eve's sobbing had stopped, and she took a hesitating breath before saying, "I hope so. I am hoping that test turns out negative."

Henri had gone straight into the shower, and when he came out, Francois was sitting in a chair waiting for him.

"What is wrong with you?" he demanded.

Henri repeated the same story to Francois. "Do you know how much it took for me not to take her in my arms and make mad, passionate love to her? I was in her bedroom, for God's sake!"

The shower had only calmed him down a little.

"It is frustrating when I have to keep looking at her and thinking she could be my sister when I have these feelings for her."

Henri sat down on the side of the bed. His shoulders slumped in defeat.

"Cheer up, buddy," Francois said, "I am sure she is just as frustrated about the whole thing as you are. I see the way she looks at you. I am positive she has the exact same feelings and frustrations. How about we focus the rest of the trip on how we can stay in the United States because without that option, these girls are lost to us. Ruth has told me that they are planning on staying here for an unknown amount of time."

Henri looked at his adopted brother with sad eyes, "You are right, Francois. Perhaps I was just a little drunk and overly tired from the day."

The next morning, at breakfast, they met some parents of children attending Notre Dame. Like the four of them, the parents seemed in no hurry and were very interested in asking them about the country of France. Ruth and Eve stayed for a lengthened conversation while Francois and Henri drove over to the University to look for the language department.

Notre Dame University is a beautiful campus built in the Gothic style, with the main building sporting a gold dome. In front was an amazingly landscaped park-like area and to the left was, obviously, a cathedral. Thinking of Ruth's instructions from her dad, Francois talked Henri into walking through the church, the Basilica of the Sacred Heart, where they marveled at the exquisite stained glass before moving on. They noticed signs to the Hasburg Library and hoped they might run into a professor there. Having struck out there, they decided to go back to the main building, hoping it housed some administrative offices where they may inquire if a language professor might be on campus.

After a short search, they found a language professor who was not too busy and willing to visit with them when he found out they were from France. He had been there several times on vacation. He asked if they had known that Notre Dame was built by a French Priest in 1842 and that all of the stained glass in the Basilica of the Sacred Heart was from French artisans. Henri and Francois appeared duly impressed and then broached the subject of their visit.

They explained to him that they were fluent in English, French, and Arabic and were trying to find out if their skills were applicable to a job in the United States in case they wanted to stay here.

He explained to them that Notre Dame used a computerized language teaching system called Mango, which provided access to 73 different languages. Most of his students were only interested in learning how to converse in the foreign language, not in reading or writing it. He said he appreciated the difficulty of writing in Arabic and that he could think of several places in America where that particular skill would be appreciated, for instance, at the United Nations Headquarters in New York or the FBI Headquarters in Washington D.C. He went on to suggest that the Wycliffe Bible Translators, with their headquarters in Orlando, Florida, would probably always welcome any foreign language writers.

They thanked him, and as they were leaving, he said, "If you give me your full names and addresses, I'll keep in touch."

Francois replied, "No, just Francois and Henri will be enough. We know how to reach you. Thanks very much, and goodbye."

When the professor got home that evening, he told his wife all about the interesting men he had met that day. He was perplexed by the fact that they wanted so much information from him but were unwilling to allow him to correspond with them if he found something for them.

She said, "That sounds very suspicious to me. They claim they are on vacation? I wonder where they are going next. If I were you, I would call the FBI and tell them all about those two men."

He didn't call, but she did.

Driving back, Henri started to laugh.

"What's so funny?" asks Francois.

"I was just thinking about Boss and the look on his face if we told him we were going to stay here and work on translating the Jewish/Christian bible. That would set him back on his heels."

Francois laughs, "You are right. How about if we told him we were going to work for the FBI?"

"Oh, we could never do anything like that," replied Henri. "He would be surprised enough if he found out we are falling in love with two Jewish girls."

When they returned, Ruth and Eve were anxious to hear their report.

"Well, what did you find out?" Ruth immediately asks Francois.

"We found some good news and some bad news." He replied. "They use a computerized language teaching system called Mango, which is capable of teaching 73 different languages, so they were not interested in our ability to teach French. However, they said that with our ability to teach Arabic writing, they might be interested in hiring one of us, but they didn't think they could find enough demand by students to need both of us," he replied.

Eve sounded amazed when she asked, "Why would they only need someone to teach written Arabic?"

"Because it is so hard to learn to write. You see, while English and French use the same letters to form each word, Arabic uses a different form of a letter depending on whether the letter is at the beginning of a word or in the middle, or at the end. Besides, Arabic is read from right to left instead of from left to right. That's why it was about a hundred years after the invention of printing that the first book was printed in Arabic," Henri patiently explained.

"Wow! Don't bother to write me anything in Arabic," Eve exclaims. "So, what did you tell them?"

"We told them we were just passing through on a vacation trip and were interested in if our language abilities would provide us with a reason to stay in the United States. They said they recommended one of two possibilities, either the United Nations in New York or the FBI," Francois replied.

"Well, at least they were helpful," Ruth volunteers in a conciliatory manner.

Francois thought it best to change the subject and asked, "What about you two? What have you been doing while we were gone?"

"We have been talking to a nice couple we met here during breakfast," Eve replies.

"The husband is Jewish, and the wife is a Christian, and they are very happily married with no religious problems at all. Their names are Ivan and Mary. It is a second marriage for both of them, and Ivan has several children from his first wife, who was Jewish, but some of them married Christians. He has no problem going to a Christian church with Mary."

Ruth, wanting to talk more seriously with Francois, took his hand and pulled him out to the balcony where they could be alone, which he took as an opportunity to kiss her and tell her he missed being away from her.

She pushed him back gently and said, "We need to talk more seriously about religion because I believe I am falling in love with you, and I seriously doubt if my father would ever stand for me marrying outside the Jewish faith."

"I guess I can understand that, but if others can do it successfully, I am sure we could too," Francois says quietly. "I am sure those Catholic Nuns who brought us up for our first five years had something else in mind." Shrugging her off, he tried to pull her close for another kiss.

"I am serious." Ruth pouted a little to see if he would open up more.

Francois sighed, took both of her hands, and said, "Honey, what religion you or our children might be is not important to me. Have you seen me stopping to turn to Mecca to pray anytime during our trip? I don't think so. Religion has always been very confusing to me. I was raised practicing the Catholic faith when I was young, then was suddenly thrown into a Muslim family. It was confusing, to say the least. In my view, I was always praying to the same God. I was just calling him by a different name. I practiced the Muslim faith while my adoptive father was alive to honor him but moved away from that faith once he passed; because, truly, it is still confusing to me. So, if, down the road, we become very, very serious and you want me to learn the Jewish faith, I will have no problem doing that. Okay?"

Ruth smiled, reached up to kiss him, and said, "Okay."

 **CHAPTER TWENTY-THREE**

Gaining Intel

It was a rainy morning in June when Susan burst into Hugh's office with a big grin on her face. She made such a noise coming in that he swiveled back around to face whoever it was and chastised them for barging in on his peaceful morning when he realized it was Susan.

Immediately he went from a faked scowl to a surprised smile and asked, "So, does rain make you happy, or is something up?"

"We almost found Francois and Henri," she says, happily

He rocks back in his chair, suspicious of such a nonsensical statement, and asked, "How can you almost find someone?"

"We know where they were yesterday. They were in South Bend, Indiana."

"Well, if one of your agents saw their car, why didn't he follow them?" he said disgustedly as he jumped to the conclusion, knowing where they were meant seeing them firsthand.

"No one saw the car," Susan smiled again at the thought of having to correct him.

"A lady called the FBI and told us her husband, who is a language professor at the University of Notre Dame, met two French professors named Francois and Henri who said they were passing through on vacation looking for a job in case they decided they wanted to stay in America. When they refused to give him their last names or forwarding address, it sounded suspicious to her, and she thought she should report it to the FBI."

Susan walked over to make herself a cup of coffee and took a seat to wait for his response.

"It's nice to know our citizens are so alert and helpful," he said as he nodded.

"What do you think we should do?" she inquired as she raised her eyebrows and looked at him over her steaming coffee.

After a pause, Hugh replied, "Well, let's think about it for a minute or two."

He sat back and began to rock his chair. Susan remained silent as she knew what Hugh was thinking. She got a kick out of watching his eyes move from left to right as if his right brain was having an argument with his left brain. Although he kept rocking, it didn't take any more than a few seconds before his eyes stopped moving, and he said, "If they are that open, they have no idea the FBI is looking for them. That's good. And if some of what they said is true, that means they probably are planning on going back to the Las Vegas airport to see that the mules are shipped as they arranged but may not plan on leaving with the mules. If you had to wait three weeks, what would you do?"

"That's very smart thinking. No wonder you are my boss. If I were them and had the opportunity to travel around sightseeing with two beautiful French girls, that is exactly what I would do. So, you think we should do nothing and just wait for them to show up?"

Nodding his head slowly while she was speaking, Hugh replied, "Exactly."

As she got up to leave, Susan had a left-brain right-brain thought of her own. *Hugh and I could take a trip to Las Vegas to intercept Francois and Henri to get all the information we can about Boss and find out if they really intend to stay in the United States. That would be great fun. I've never been to Las Vegas. Maybe, on the other hand, I should probably not mention it just yet. But I can always hope for it.*

Hugh watched her as she changed facial expressions on her way out but decided not to ask what those were all about. Whatever it was, he was sure she would let him know if he needed to know.

 # CHAPTER TWENTY-FOUR

Brett

Henri was not in a better mood when he got up the next morning. He joined the others downstairs in the common area for a breakfast of pancakes and sausage. After some obligatory good morning greetings, he asked, "Where are we headed today?"

Ruth responded that they were traveling from Indiana through Ohio to their last destination, which is Fallingwater near Pittsburg in Pennsylvania.

They all agreed that it would be faster to take the main highways, which would give Francois and Henri more time to visit colleges and universities along the way and for Ruth to observe the architecture.

They studied the maps they had and made detailed plans to take Interstate highways and visit Toledo, Ohio and Lourdes College, Cleveland, Ohio and Baldwin-Wallace College, Youngstown, Ohio and Youngstown State University, Grove City, Pennsylvania and Grove City College, Slippery Rock, Pennsylvania and Slippery Rock University of Pennsylvania, Pittsburgh Pennsylvania and Washington and Jefferson College then take route 40 to California University of Pennsylvania and finally to their last destination, a home by Frank Lloyd Wright designated Fallingwater. They would then drive back to the Pittsburgh airport and fly back to Las Vegas, Nevada.

"I hope the results of the DNA test will be waiting for us when we get back to Las Vegas," said Henri, the frustration and impatience evident in his voice.

He looked at Eve, who was feeling so conflicted she hadn't said a word and barely looked at him the entire time they were having breakfast. As they got up to leave, Ruth volunteered to drive the first leg of the trip, and Eve quickly volunteered to sit up front and navigate. Realizing something was amiss with Henri and Eve, neither Ruth nor Francois objected.

Each time they met people at breakfast, they tried to turn the conversion to religion and ask if anyone knew a couple that had an inter-faith marriage.

Henri decided to break the silence on the drive by stirring up the conversation about a man named Brett that they had met at breakfast that morning. The tension dissipated as they all began to talk about what they had learned from this man who had been brought up as a Southern Baptist and married an Episcopalian.

When Brett was a teenager, he was in love with a Catholic girl. He thought she was in love with him, but although they were making big plans for their future, she was also dating someone else. He became so infuriated that he took a picture she had given him, nailed it up on a tree, and shot it full of holes with his BB gun.

They laughed as they retold this part of his story but were then equally tsk-tsking when they recounted that because of this slight from a love interest, he began to hate all Catholics.

"He must have been quite a hot-tempered sort," Eve exclaimed.

"Yes, and apparently very decisive," Henri added. "It struck me as odd that he simply changed his first name to his mother's maiden name just because he didn't like his first name."

They each shared their feelings about the importance of naming a child and then picked back up with their recollection of Brett's story.

Brett later married an Episcopalian over the objections of his family. In those days, where they lived, in Charleston, South Carolina, there was some animosity between different Christian religions. His family thought he had "gone to hell" by marrying an Episcopalian. Brett went to church with his wife and brought up their children as Episcopalians. However, Brett only went to church on Christmas and Easter. Although his twice-a-year "heathen" activities seemed to ease tensions with his side of the family, they only truly reconciled when the children came into their lives.

As if the Baptist/Episcopalian merger wasn't enough to contend with, the next turmoil Brett had to go through was when he found that his only son was going to marry a Catholic girl. He cried at the wedding. It was probably the only time he had been inside a Catholic church.

He only became reconciled when his first grandson was born. He was elated when his first grandchild was a son and carried his name. He often bragged to his golfing buddies, "You should show me a little more respect. After all, you may sometime discover that you have been playing with the grandfather of the Pope."

They all laughed as they recalled this last part of Brett's story and all tension seemed to have escaped from the car for the rest of the drive.

 **CHAPTER TWENTY-FIVE**

Plan B Created

Tom arrived in Algiers after a stop in London to mail one of his postcards. He met with his Vets and brought them up to speed on the overall program and how they are going to work, including how to install the latest design of listening devices that can be read and reset remotely. He emphasized that this must be done as soon as possible after the two mules arrive in case they are to be rented immediately. The vets were connected with animal quarantine and agreed to do their part during the 14-day quarantine period.

They discussed the need for Plan B in case the man known as the Boss became suspicious.

One of his Vets suggested that they create a diversion by installing one of their old-style listening devices on a horse. This was a device that was small enough to be installed on the side of a horse's hoof but has no memory and recording capability but must be attached to an antenna running up the horse's leg. He pointed out that it can be set to buzz, which would cause the horse to stamp his foot, assuring them to find it at a pre-selected time.

One of the vets objected, "But wouldn't this mean they would kill the horse and accuse you of bugging it?"

"We would have to devise a scheme to be able to prove our innocence, but it may involve sacrificing the horse," he replied and went on to say. "Fortunately, there will be a big horse auction in town a few days from now. If we get some horses from there and use them for our fake listening devices, we can claim we had nothing to do with installing them, that they must have been installed by others before we got them."

"Great. That's our plan B," they all agreed.

 # CHAPTER TWENTY-SIX

Size Should Matter

Early July in Toledo, Ohio, was hot enough that Ruth was glad she rented a car with an air conditioner. As they drove through town, they were taken aback by the litter they saw on the street.

"Perhaps the garbage men are on strike," Eve exclaimed.

It was already past 4 when they arrived in Toledo, so they decided to try and find the Country Inn and Suites.

The couple they had met in South Bend had come through Toledo and highly recommended a Bread and Breakfast there called Country Inn and Suites. They were delighted that they did because, at breakfast, they found they each had the chance to make their favorite kind of waffle. Ruth made a waffle with strawberries mixed in, while Eve chose blueberries.

"Amateurs," Francois teased as he made his banana, strawberry, and pecan waffle which was so big that it dripped out the sides of the waffle iron.

Henri shook his head in disgust at the mess Francois had made and moved to the other waffle iron, where he expertly made his pecan waffle.

The breakfast room had a number of small, separate tables, each seating four people, but they were close enough together that it was easy to start a conversation with the tourists at the next table.

They asked about colleges there in Toledo and were told that the most famous one nearby was Lourdes

University in Sylvania, Ohio, just northwest of downtown Toledo. It is a Catholic college operated by a group of Nuns called The Sisters of Saint Francis.

After getting directions, they decided to drive through it on their way to Cleveland just to see what the architecture was like. As they approached the entrance to the college, they were all greatly impressed by the beautiful homes they passed.

Ruth remarked, "I think this area is what the Americans call the "high-rent district." She was probably right because the college was located between the Sylvania Country Club and the Highland Meadows Golf Club. They were all amazed at the beautiful homes, all three-story mansions with a mixture of colonial and modern architecture. However, they turned in to the entrance to the college only to be disappointed by the plain, sparse, but economic appearance of the buildings. The university was much smaller than Notre Dame. Francois and Henri commented that the mission-style architecture reminded them of the Catholic orphanage where they grew up.

They found a parking space, and they all got out to walk around the campus. The campus was much smaller than Notre Dame, and they soon realized that walking around the outside of the campus was about all they could do because the doors were locked, and nobody seemed to be around. They made their way back to the main common area in front of the administration building and stood there for a minute, silently looking at it.

Ruth popped up with, "All right, so much for that. Let's head for Cleveland."

As they returned through Toledo, Ruth spotted the Franklin Park Mall and suggested they stop there so that she and Eve could do a little shopping. Francois pulled into a convenient parking place and asked, "How long do you think you will be?"

"I suppose about an hour or so. Why don't we meet you back here at the car in an hour?" Ruth suggested.

"That will be fine. You go ahead. I want to look for a book store to learn some more about the United States," Francois replied.

Walking through the shopping mall with Henri, Francois found just what he was looking for, a bookstore that sold textbooks. First, he found a U.S.A. History book, then a geography book with information about all 50 states. The book store also contained a large world globe on a stand. They stopped beside it and turned it around so they could see the United States to the left and Europe to the right.

"You see what I mean?" Francois asked. "If you placed the outline of the United States over Europe, it would cover all of Europe and the Mediterranean Sea plus a lot of North Africa."

"That's amazing. No wonder people in Europe and Africa don't understand how big the U.S.A. is," Henri replied, shaking his head.

They went straight back to the car and started thumbing through the books. Francois had the geography book. He turned to Henri and said, "You know that the size of France is a little more than 247 thousand square miles. Well, the the state of Texas is more than 268 thousand square miles. And another thing, the population's table shows that the combined populations of California and Texas are larger than that of France. It's amazing. I had no idea that the United States was so big, and I am sure Boss doesn't either."

With his eyebrows raised, Henri asks, "So, what's the point?"

"The point is we need the United States to be our friend, not our enemy."

Francois flipped the pages to one showing a map of the whole United States and said to Henri, "Take a look at this map. Do you see this small state called North Carolina? The population of that state is almost exactly the same as the population of Israel."

"So, what?"

"What that means is, if the United States really wanted to help Israel in a war, all they would have to do is round up their young, able-bodied men in that one state and send them to Israel, and they would double the size of their army."

"Wow, that is impressive. I think he would understand that, but would he believe it? That's part of the problem," Henri says.

"Here is another way to explain to Boss how futile his thinking is," counters Francois.

Taking out another little book on populations that he had been carrying around, Francois said, "Take a look at this book on the population of the various countries and suppose you wanted to decide whether you wanted the United States to be a friend or foe. With its 325 million people, it has a population equal to Israel, Spain, France, Italy, the United Kingdom, and Germany combined. Would you like to have all of those countries against you?" Francois points out.

He goes on to say, "It's just plain stupid to think you can injure the United States by knocking down a couple of large buildings, even if they are full of people. The only thing you can possibly accomplish is to make over 320 million people mad at you."

"That makes a much more convincing argument," Henri agreed.

 # CHAPTER TWENTY-SEVEN

Tension

Just then, Ruth and Eve returned, and they were off again. They discussed the fact that it would be too early to stop for the night when they reached Cleveland, so they agreed to a little side trip.

Taking the turn-off to Avon Lake, they decide to investigate a Bed and Breakfast there which had been recommended to them. It turned out to be a very pretty little home near the beach at Lake Erie, which would have provided a view of beautiful sunsets, but they didn't stop.

They returned to Interstate 90 and continued through the downtown area of Cleveland. To their surprise, they realized they must be passing Cleveland State University when they saw a huge tower to their left, which was its hallmark. It was a huge square grey tower, over 15 stories high, 40 or 50 feet on either side. It was quite beautiful and stood out impressively, dwarfing all the buildings in the area.

"Look at that," said Ruth, "We are at Cleveland State University! There's a different approach to university architecture. Maybe we should consider a building like that for our three religions, one on each floor."

"And you could design it so that when you wanted to add another religion, you just added another floor," Francois suggested happily.

Eve chimed in, "And best of all, it would be religion-neutral, so it wouldn't offend anyone."

"That's exactly right. We'll have to discuss it with dad. I can hear him now saying, 'Where does Frank Lloyd Wright's influence come in?'"

As they were talking about that, Ruth pulled out the map and said, "Wait a minute, stop; we have to turn around. We are heading to the wrong road. We were supposed to switch from Interstate 95 to Interstate 80 to get to Pittsburg. We'll have to go back."

Francois, who was driving, calmly took the next exit ramp and quipped, "Okay, which way, navigator?"

"Just get back on I90 and exit going south on I77 until you see I80 east," Ruth responded.

As they go past Cleveland State University again, Ruth says, "That was a lucky mistake. If we had turned onto Interstate 80 back where we should have, we would have missed seeing any of this, including Avon Lake."

As they traveled along Interstate 80 going east, Ruth reminded Francois that he needed to turn south on Interstate 79 to go to Pittsburgh. When he did, Eve pulled out her cellphone and busily started trying different things.

"What are you working so hard at?" said Henri.

"I think it's time that we found a good French restaurant. I'm sure there must be one in Pittsburgh," she replied.

"Good idea."

"So far, I have found 15 restaurants that claim to serve French food. I am trying to narrow it down."

"Maybe we should stay a few days and see how many we could try."

"I think I have it narrowed down to two. There is Poulet Bleu which advertises 'classic French fare,' and Café Du Jour, which says they have a 'romantic patio.' Which do you think you would prefer?"

A loud chorus of "Both," was heard from three voices.

"Surely, if we are going to fly out of here after we visit Fallingwater, we will have plenty of time to visit several restaurants."

"My thoughts exactly," Ruth said. "Let's start with the romantic patio. Do you have the address?"

"Yes. 1107 East Carson Street."

"Good. I also want to try staying overnight at what I understand is one of the most popular places for tourists to stay, which is a Holiday Inn Express and Suites. We need to do something to get more acclimated to American ways by learning more of their customs if we expect to have a good business here," said Ruth.

"That's a very good thought. We could take one of their suites and continue with one of our own newfound customs," replied Francois.

They checked into a large suite that held two separate bedrooms, one with a king-size bed in it and the other with two queens. Each bedroom had an adjoining shower. Between the bedrooms was a large sitting room with a fridge and mini-bar, a sofa, a table, four chairs, and a desk area with available Wi-Fi.

Eve noticed that there was an indoor swimming pool and announced that she was going to put on her new bathing suit and take a swim before dinner. Ruth volunteered to join her, but before Francois could say anything, Henri put his hand on his shoulder and asked him to go to the weight room that he had spied on the first floor. The girls went into the room with the king-sized bed to change, so Francois and Henri retreated to the other room.

The water felt refreshingly cool but not cold as Eve and Ruth swam lazily around for several minutes relaxing in the weightlessness. Eve did not seem her usual happy self. In fact, she had been rather quiet all day. Finally, Ruth asked what was wrong.

"I'm just sad," Eve said with a heavy sigh, "Henri and I had such a strong attraction for each other, but every time you and Francois leave us to go off on your own, things become tense. I am confused about what to do. How to act. That DNA test has come between us. One part of me wants so badly to throw caution to the wind and treat him like a lover, but the other part of me keeps reminding me to keep my distance because he could be my brother. It's not easy trying to hold in my emotions because the more I get to know him. I just love everything about him."

"It must be awfully frustrating for you," Ruth sympathized. "How about tonight, after dinner, you break out those cards you had on the airplane, and we play pinochle or hearts, or spades, or something until we get sleepy. I won't try to sneak away with Francois, and tomorrow, after we visit Falling Waters, we will be headed to the airport. Hopefully, when we get back to the hotel in Las Vegas, there will be an answer for us from the DNA you sent off."

Eve shook her head in agreement and gave off a heavy sigh again, "At first, I was hoping he was my brother, but now I am wishing he is not."

Ruth smiled and gave her sister a hug. "I'm sure everything will be alright," she assured her.

In the gym, Francois and Henri were running on treadmills, not saying a word to each other.

"What is up with you, Henri? You seem to have been in a foul mood for days," he said accusingly as he kept running.

"Oh, I guess I'm just jealous of the relationship you have with Ruth," Henri replied as he shut off his treadmill and went over to the universal weight machine.

Francois had also ran enough and had no desire to work out further, so he sat down on one of the workout benches close to Henri, a little confused.

"Really, I thought you and Eve were getting along very well. Are you still bothered by the other night?" he asked.

"Even though I took that DNA test, I never believed I was her brother, so I let myself enjoy her company as I would any girl. But the more time we spent together, the more I grew to love her. The problem is now that I love her, I am concerned for her, and the fact that the damn DNA test may show that we are related! I have such a strong attraction to her that every time you and Ruth leave us to go off on our own, things become tense. I am confused about what to do and how to act. Because I am concerned for her, I don't want to throw caution to the wind and let my true feelings out. That damn DNA test has come between us! And you know, brother, not that I would want to cramp your style, but leaving Eve and me alone while you and Ruth go off is not helping things."

Defiantly, Francois stood up and started to scold Henri like a little schoolboy, "I'm not sorry I've stolen some time with Ruth alone," he started then changed his tune when, instead of thinking of other things to defend himself with, he put himself in Henri's shoes. "But," he continued, "I suppose it is rather frustrating to be in love with someone who might turn out to be your sister. Quite a conflict of emotions."

"Yes, and now we are staying in the same suite with them instead of separate rooms." Henri let out a frustrated, "Ach!"

"Okay, calm down. We will just have to think of something so that we entertain them until they get sleepy."

Francois thought for a minute and continued, "We had a good time playing cards the first time we stayed in the same suite with them. How about we suggest playing cards after dinner?"

Henri thought this was a good idea and finally let the weights down with a gentle thud. When they passed the door to the swimming-pool, they saw that the girls were already gone, so they hurried back to the suite to take a shower and change.

Once on the flight back to Las Vegas, Ruth commented, "That Fallingwater was certainly a beautiful home and a magnificent setting, but I don't think any of it applies to our design problem. I've got so many new design ideas popping into my head that I'm anxious to get to a drawing board where I can try them out."

"Which of the things we have seen made the most impressions on you?" says Francois.

"Two of them, the plain, unadorned church and the big tower at The University of Cleveland."

Eve said, "I'm also anxious to get back to Las Vegas and go to work finding an office for us in a good location downtown. I wonder if there are any good French restaurants in Las Vegas."

Francois and Henri both comment that they enjoyed the trip so much that they were reluctant to end it.

CHAPTER TWENTY-EIGHT

Competition

Hugh was sitting at his desk, going over some notes he made the night before when Susan came storming in, trying to catch her breath.

"We have some interesting news from our agent in Las Vegas. There is someone else looking for Francois and Henri besides us," she said anxiously as she marched in and plopped down in the closest chair to Hugh. She leaned over toward him, which startled Hugh. Dropping his pen, he pushed back his chair and asked, "Really, how does he know?"

"It all happened in one day, yesterday," she says, undaunted by his attempt to dampen her enthusiasm. "He got a call from his friend in Tusayan saying there was a man there asking whether two men named Francois and Henri had bought any mules. He told him they were there, couldn't buy any but leased two, which were scheduled to be shipped to Algiers soon. However, the plane became available earlier than expected, so they were shipped a few days ago. Apparently, either that same man or someone else showed up later the same day at the Las Vegas Paris Hotel, asking if Francois and Henri were checked in. When he was told no, but they were expected back, he gave the desk clerk an envelope to hold for them when they arrived."

"What did they say the man looked like?" Hugh quickly asked.

"They said there was nothing noticeable about him, just average in every way," Susan replied, slowly shaking her head.

"That's very helpful. We can stop looking for them; just wait for them to come to us," Hugh said as he picked his pen back up to resume what he was working on before she came in.

"And that sounds like just what you anticipated. Very clever," Susan said, smiling in admiration.

"Is your guy in Vegas keeping tabs on the man with the envelope?" Hugh asked offhandedly, still correcting his paperwork.

"I'll check on that," Susan said and quickly left to make the call.

CHAPTER TWENTY-NINE

Las Vegas

The hotel Paris, expecting Eve and Ruth's return, had a room ready for them along with some mail. While Francois and Henri checked in, the attendant recalled some instructions from his supervisor and asked them to wait a moment. He went to the back and quickly returned with an envelope that Francois shoved in his pocket before anyone noticed.

After making plans for dinner, they went to their separate rooms.

Once behind closed doors, Francois quickly opened the envelope and found it contained two credit cards and an unsigned letter written in Arabic. Startled, he read it to Henri, "Thank you for sending the two mules. You have done a great job. We have decided to proceed without doing any language training. It is not needed. Your pay and your severance pay have both been placed in these two credit card accounts. Have a nice vacation, and I will see you when you get home. No signature. P.S. Stay out of the casinos."

"That must mean they sent the mules while we were away," Francois concluded.

"This is absolutely amazing! That also means we are free to do whatever we want. We can even go to the casinos now. Something I have wanted to do," Henri said eagerly. "It had to be hand-delivered! You don't suppose Boss actually came to America as a result of what we have been writing him, do you?"

"No, I am sure he must have sent one of our other two brothers. They are the only ones he would trust to do this. He must have decided to change his plans and concentrate his efforts directly on the Israelis."

"Let's go see the girls."

At the same time, Ruth and Eve were opening all the mail left for them.

When Eve came to the letter from the DNA testing company, she turned white as a sheet, and started to tremble. Handing the envelope to Ruth, she whispers, "You better open this. I'm too scared."

Ruth opened the letter and read it.

Letting out a loud laugh, she proclaims, "You have a brother. It's Francois!"

"Wow! Fantastic!"

Laughing and crying at the same time, they hugged each other and jumped up and down with joy.

As they separated, Eve became concerned, "But suppose he doesn't like it."

"Don't worry; he'll love it. I know he will. I know him well now, well enough to love him."

Just then, there is a knock on the door. Ruth opened it and pulled Francois excitedly inside. Eve saw Henri and ran excitedly into his arms. "I hope you won't be disappointed, but you are not my brother."

Henri let out an obvious sigh of relief and hugged her closer. After he released her from his embrace, she turned to Ruth and Francois, who just finished a long kiss. "Ahem," Eve faked a loud cough to break them apart. "Francois, how would you feel about having a sister?" she asked shyly.

"What's this?" he asked.

"The DNA test came back showing that you and I are brother and sister. Is that okay?"

"Perfect!" Henri and Francois exclaimed in unison.

"I believe we have a lot of celebrating to do tonight!" Francois exclaimed.

"Actually, if you don't mind, I've waited long enough for some alone time with Eve," Henri said as he quickly looked around and then led her to the balcony. Shutting the drapes behind him, he called back, "And I am sure you have some things to say to Ruth."

He took Eve in his arms and started, "Eve..." but he was cut off.

"Oh, shut up and kiss me," Eve demanded.

He was not used to being interrupted, but he looked into her beautiful blue eyes, smiled, and slowly lowered his lips towards hers. They were nose to nose when he softly said, "I'm so glad you are not my sister," then gave her small, soft kisses on her lips, her cheeks, her eyelids, the side of her face, and her neck before returning to her lips again to kiss her long and passionately. Every fiber of her being tingled with excitement. "I love you, and you know that, don't you?" he whispered.

"Yes," she answered, "and I love you also."

"I have news for you, but Francois and I need to run a couple of errands to confirm some things so we can be sure; how about if I pick you up for dinner around 7?" he said softly as he continued to kiss her.

"I am all yours," she responded.

He opened the door back into the suite to find Ruth and Francois close together, talking softly.

"Are you ready to run our errands?" Henri asked.

Francois kissed Ruth one more time as he got up from the couch and said, "Yep, we are on a mission, brother. See you at 7, sweetheart." He said to Ruth as they left.

Francois and Henri discovered that the two credit cards were actually debit cards for accounts at a local bank. They went directly to the bank to present the cards and check on the balance in their accounts. Each account held $150,000. Their next stop was at a jewelry store, where they both made purchases.

They then went back to their hotel, where they called the local courthouse and confirmed that in Las Vegas, all they needed to get married was a marriage license and a valid passport. The marriage license would be good for 30 days.

They agreed that they would take the girls out separately and meet up later, hopefully for after-dinner drinks and a celebration.

As brothers do, they argued over who was going to which restaurant and drew straws. Francois and Ruth would dine at the Eiffel Tower Restaurant, and Henri would take Eve to the Mon Ami Gabbi Restaurant. They picked the girls up precisely at 7:00. Henri and Francois were polite, but somehow the girls felt there was a nervous quietness about them. When Francois punched the 'up' elevator button, and Henri punched the 'down' button, the girls looked at them curiously.

"It's time for a little alone dining time," Francois said, as he gave a wink and a nod to Henri, who returned the gesture. The girls' eyes lit up, and they smiled broadly at each other.

"Well, today is full of surprises," teased Ruth.

As they were waiting for their first course, Francois could not contain himself.

"I have something for you, Ruth, my dear," he started.

She took a sip of water and gave him her complete attention.

"I have told you that I love you, and I grow to love you more and more each day I am with you. In fact, I don't want to spend another day without you. I think about you when I go to sleep, and you are my first thought when I wake up. I am planning on starting a new adventure here in America. I don't have it all worked out yet other than the fact that I need you with me, and I want you to marry me," he pulled a small black ring box out of his pocket, put it on the table, and pushed it towards her.

She opened the box to a large emerald-cut diamond ring. "YES!" she cried. "I will marry you. I feel exactly the same way about you!" then she paused.

"But you will have to ask my father for his blessing."

Francois took both her hands in his and became quite solemn.

"No problem, my love. I will move both heaven and earth for you."

She leaned across the table to kiss him as he took the box back and placed the ring on her finger. They ordered champagne, and he began to tell her about the fact that he did not have to go back to Algiers at all so if she was going to be here in Las Vegas, then he would start looking for work here also.

At the Mon Ami Gabbi, Henri and Eve had lots to talk about. They both explained why they had been so nervous and uneasy around each other towards the end of the trip and how difficult it was to hold their feelings in. What Eve had read as Henri's being mad at her was the same real sexual tension, she had been feeling for him. She was glad they waited and stayed at arm's length; it made her respect Henri all the more.

He told her that their initial plans to return to Algiers had altered and confirmed that enough money had been wired to them as severance pay to last them for a year or more. He told her that she was the most beautiful girl he had ever seen. As he reached into his pocket, he told her that he loved her wit, he loved her personality, he loved her spirit, and he felt he had found his soulmate. Then he moved from his seat to kneel on one knee beside her, opened the small box to reveal a beautiful marquise cut diamond, and asked her to marry him.

She flung her arms around him, kissing him and saying, "Yes, yes, yes. Stand up, please. You are making a scene." He stood up, put the ring on her finger, and they kissed again while all of the diners and staff around them applauded.

After dinner, they met Francois and Ruth at The Napolean's Lounge.

Henri couldn't wait to tell Francois that he and Eve had stopped by a casino.

"I think she must have some Scottish blood in her," he said to Francois. "As soon as we got a hundred dollars ahead, she insisted on stopping and cashing in."

"We found out that foreigners could get married in Las Vegas with just a marriage license and a valid passport," Francois informed the girls. "Now that we are one big happy family, we should get married and make it official."

"I need to call my dad and tell him the good news. He will certainly want to fly over for the wedding," said Ruth, a little more thoughtfully. "It is too late in France. I will have to wait until he is up and has had breakfast. He will be in a good mood then and better able to handle all this news."

"Then let's get back to the room because, at 10:00 p.m., it will be 8:00 a.m. there," Eve chimed in.

They rushed back to the girl's suite and ordered a bottle of champagne and four glasses.

As soon as the champagne was poured, Eve announced, "This would be a good time for us to plan our honeymoons. Should we go together or go to separate places?"

A long discussion ensued in which they all agreed they might as well stick together since they planned to be one big happy family. Henri pointed out that they needn't go far since there were plenty of French restaurants in Las Vegas.

"I have a suggestion," Ruth said. "Remember, on our first dinner date, you said you were going to drive out to the Grand Canyon, that it would probably be an overnight trip, and would we like to come along? Why don't we make that trip? I would love to see the Grand Canyon."

"That's a great idea," Eve concurred. "What was the hotel where you stayed?"

"We didn't pay much attention to the hotel's name. I remember it was in the little town of Tusayan, Arizona. We should be able to look it up," Francois commented.

Eve had her cell phone out and was punching it in. "Here's one, the Grand Hotel. Does that sound like it?"

"That's it! The Grand Hotel at The Grand Canyon is how they advertise it. By the way, there is a little airport there at Tusayan in case you would rather fly. Unless you want to stop and visit Hoover Dam on the way, it would be a long and slightly boring trip by car. It's the trip where we were surprised that we just breezed across the state lines without having to stop and show our passports," Francois remembered.

They all agreed that they had enough of riding in a car for a while and decided that Francois would take care of the plane and hotel reservations when the exact date and time were set.

 # CHAPTER THIRTY

Permission Delayed

Ruth waited until she thought it was the best time to call her dad. She knew that after he had had breakfast and was relaxing with his newspaper and a second cup of coffee at home in Paris, it would be about 11:30 their time.

"Hello, dad. I hope you are sitting down with your second cup of coffee because I have lots of news to tell you. You're on the speaker, so we can all hear you."

"You're right. I am," he says, glad to hear his daughter's voice again.

"I'll start with Eve. All that work with DNA has paid off. She has found a brother. Actually, he's only a half-brother, but according to the DNA test, they have the same mother. We are all delighted. It's Francois."

"Isn't that one of the guys you have been traveling with?"

"Yes, it is. And she has fallen in love with the other one, Henri, and they are going to be married."

"But we know who her mother is or was," by this time, he had dropped his newspaper, stood up abruptly, and was pacing the floor.

"Yes, we have been talking about that. Remember when I told you that Henri and Francois were both orphans, born in a Catholic hospital and orphanage in Algiers. You probably remember that years ago, when an unmarried girl in Paris became pregnant, one of her options was to go to Algiers to have the baby. It could be born and brought up there at the orphanage."

Her father paused for a moment to think about how he was going to reply and, finally, said, "Yes, I remember that. So, that's probably what happened. DNA science is wonderful, but you don't always like what you learn. Apparently, in this case, we do. What about Francois? What does he think about this?"

"He loves it. Here is the next big news. He and I are in love, and he wants to marry me. But I told him that he would have to ask you for my hand."

"Wait, wait, you are going too fast for me. Let me sit down for a minute. Are you telling me you are thinking of marrying someone that I haven't even met and that you have only known for a few weeks?! How could all this happen the first time you go away from home?"

"That's what I am saying. You need to come over here and meet him. Also, you need to sell my new design plans for the College of Religions to your clients."

"You have some new plans already? Your trip must have paid off. What did you learn?"

"First, I learned that three different buildings are not practical. It's going to be hard enough to recruit students to the college without requiring them to enter strange buildings. One neutral building, like one of Frank Lloyd Wright's, would be a better choice."

"What would it look like?"

"It would look a lot like the first one I saw in New York. I haven't gotten the design on paper yet, but it will be unique, like some of his. It would be a round tower that could be added to in height, each religion occupying a floor. We could start with three floors, but it would probably be better to start with five if we could afford it. A unique feature would be that access to each floor would be by stairs on the outside surrounding the building to give the overall feeling of openness to the different religions."

"That sounds pretty good. You're right. I certainly do need to come over there as soon as I can. I hope you haven't started planning a wedding ceremony yet."

"No, we haven't. That depends on when they each get jobs and arrange to stay in the United States. But wait, I have some good news for you about your trip over here."

"Oh, what is that?"

"While we were visiting the various buildings designed by Frank Lloyd Wright as you instructed, several times people asked us if we had been to Florida. We told them no, why, and they said there is one place there where you can see over a dozen of Frank Lloyd Wright's buildings all in one place. It seems that he was commissioned to design the campus of Florida Southern College in Lakeland, Florida. So, you need to tell your travel agent to route you through Lakeland, Florida, on your way from Paris to Las Vegas. We looked it up on our maps which shows you would probably have to fly into either Tampa or Orlando, Florida, and rent a car to drive back and forth to Lakeland because it is a small town."

"That sounds great. I would love to see that. I think I would want to spend a couple of days there to take it all in. Maybe I will follow your lead and stay at a Bed and Breakfast where I should be able to meet some Americans. Do you think I should take along an interpreter? My English is not so good."

"Oh, I think it will be good enough. I wouldn't worry about that."

"Okay. Keep me posted on your schedule. Meantime, I will contact my travel agent and start brushing up on my English. Goodbye for now."

He put the phone down and sat back in his favorite chair with a big sigh, saying to himself, "Wow, things are happening so fast it's almost enough to drive me to drink."

 # CHAPTER THIRTY-ONE

Job Offer

The mid-July sun was blistering hot. While the girls were out looking for office space, they also shopped for light summer dresses, sandals, and plenty of sunscreen. Francois and Henri started looking for jobs in and around Las Vegas.

They first went to the University of Nevada in downtown Las Vegas and quickly discovered that there was a suburb of Las Vegas called Henderson that contained quite a few colleges and universities located to the southeast. After talking to a professor in the language department, they drove down route 582 to Henderson.

On the way, they decided to discuss only their ability to teach French because they were sure nobody would be interested in learning Arabic.

They visited the Nevada State College, the College of Southern Nevada, and DeVry University.

Each time they got the same response; not only did the college have no openings in those subjects, but they each had a backlog of applicants from those countries wanting to move to Las Vegas and teach those subjects.

Finally, when they visited DeVry University, they asked about teaching Arabic. It was suggested to them that if they were fluent in that language, they were on the wrong end of town, and they should go in a direction northeast of Las Vegas to talk to the personnel director at Nellis Air Force Base.

Discouraged, they went back to the hotel, relaxed, and discussed their concerns about applying for a job at a military base. After much arguing back and forth, in desperation, they decided to go ahead and give it a try. After all, what could they lose? They still assumed that nobody in the United States knew who they were.

They drove to Nellis Air Force Base, stopping at the entrance gate and asking the guard there for an appointment to see the personnel director to apply for a job.

As they waited anxiously in the car, the guard telephoned the Personnel Director to explain the situation. Luckily, he was not busy and agreed to see them right away.

Tentatively, they explained their situation to him; that they were in the United States on vacation, both expected to be married soon, and were fully qualified to teach French and Arabic.

He was delighted to see them. As he shook their hands, he explained, "You two are just what I am looking for. My problem is that all my foreign language experts only know one foreign language, and that gives me many scheduling problems."

They stared at each other as their jaws dropped. They were amazed at their luck. He motioned them to a couple of chairs. They sat on the edges of their chairs, listening intently to every word.

"Here is how our system works. You will be given a small class of up to six students that are scheduled to be transferred to a foreign country. You will be required to teach them not only the foreign language but also the customs of the people in that country. When they graduate and move, you will be required to go with them to live and work in the U.S. Embassy in that country. You will be working for the U.S Government as a civil servant assigned to the Air Force. While assigned there for a period of up to three months, you will report to our Ambassador. Then you will return to Las Vegas and start the process over again. How does that sound to you?"

"What about our families?"

"That's the only drawback. You will have to leave them here for two reasons; there is only one space available at the embassy, and we need the assurance that you will come back and not be tempted to do otherwise."

"What will we be doing at the embassy?"

"You will continue to teach your trainees. You will read the local daily newspapers and bring them up to speed on all the local news, especially sports, economics, and politics. This will continue until they are familiar with the local customs, are able to read the local newspaper, and have met two or three local natives. Then you will come back here, have a week or two off, and start the whole process over again."

"How about pay?"

"You will start at a fairly low salary and, if your work is satisfactory, you will be given a raise each time you return to the states. If you would like to complete these applications and they prove satisfactory, I can start you a week from Monday."

They are both stunned and stare at each other, trying to think of something to say.

Finally, Francois spoke.

"We are both about to get married. Before we accept, do you think we could have some time to talk this over with our fiancés?"

"I wouldn't have it any other way. Shall we say tomorrow morning at 9 o'clock?"

"Thank you very much. We'll be back."

With that, they got up and left, quietly, slowly, walking out like they were walking on eggshells. Once outside, they almost ran to their car, eager to look closely at the application forms to make sure there would be no pitfalls.

Riding back to the hotel, they were both almost too stunned to talk. Finally, Francois said, "Some of this is almost too good to be true, but, on the other hand, how can we take a job that requires us to leave the country? The girls would never stand for that."

"But he said he would help us get our citizenship. That's worth a lot."

"We will just have to talk it over with Ruth and Eve. Maybe we can get him to let us work in this country long enough to satisfy them. It's too good an opportunity to pass up," concluded Henri.

 **CHAPTER THIRTY-TWO**

Francois and Henri Uncovered

Hugh expected Friday to be a casual day as he leisurely checked in at the CIA's main gate at 9:00 a.m., expecting to leave early for some afternoon golf. When he walked in, he found Susan waiting for him at his office door.

"Good morning," he said cheerfully. "You look very bright-eyed. What's happening?"

"A lot," she replied confidently, "I couldn't wait to tell you. Francois and Henri have applied for a job at Nellis Air Force Base! They want us to tell them whether or not they should be considered a security risk. Nellis has a Special Operations school for foreign languages that sometimes hire foreign nationals to train Air Force Officers."

"Yes, I know about that school. Some of those officers are qualified to work in our foreign embassies," Hugh replied calmly. "We need to think that over carefully. Tell them to just hold off for a few days while we gather some more information."

He waits while Susan makes her phone call and relays the message. As soon as she puts down her phone, Hugh says, "Sit down. Let's review what we know. Francois and Henri were sent here to obtain some mules for someone called Boss, who is trying to train suicide bombers. While they were here, they found that they had some time on their hands, so they took a sightseeing trip with Ruth and Eve, who apparently came here permanently to work and live.

Recently, someone came looking for Francois and Henri, left them something, and now they are looking for a job. Why? Was he giving them a new job? Or was he firing them? What do you think?"

"You left out how they acted," Susan pointed out. "The first odd act was not going to any casinos. Then our agent, who was observing them, reported that at dinner, they seemed to be very intimate. I think they may have fallen in love. They sure spent a lot of time together on that trip. Maybe they just want to stay in the USA."

"You may have just solved our problem. Not going to a casino is a big clue," said Hugh. "I think they were instructed to stay out of casinos to avoid being photographed. If that is the case and the messenger came to fire them because they don't need them anymore, they should start going to casinos now."

"Great! That's right! I'll discuss it with our observer," Susan agreed as she finished making her cup of coffee.

"No, we don't need to discuss it," Hugh replied sternly as he pulls out a large, yellow legal notepad and starts to write. "I'll write down our response so there will be no chance of any misinterpretation."

Hugh wrote:

"With regard to the two men, Francois Allard and Henri Blanchet, who are language professors from the University of Algiers.

They were sent to the United States on an errand to obtain trained riding mules for a group we now know to be attempting to recruit and train suicide bombers. Having completed that mission, they apparently have been discharged from that group because their services are no longer needed. Currently, they are about to be married to two French women they met here and have applied for work at Nellis AFB. The CIA recommends that they be denied any access to classified information and/or any access to American Embassies in any foreign country. Please be advised that we will continue to request the FBI to monitor their location and activities."

Hugh then signed the note, tore off the sheet, and handed it to Susan, who read it quickly, nodding as she did, glanced at Hugh, who was watching her, and left for her office.

At the same time this was happening, Francois, Henri, Ruth, and Eve were in a long discussion about the job offers they had received. They finally all agreed that although very tempting, particularly the part about assisting them in becoming citizens, they would respectively decline it and look for something else.

At 3:30, Hugh knocked on Susan's door and peeked in.

"I am taking off for the day to have a 'business golf meeting.' If you would like to meet me at the Country Club around 6:30, I'd be glad to give you another golf lesson and take you to dinner afterward."

Susan looked up from her laptop and smiled that beautiful smile at him.

"Why that sounds like a lovely way to spend a Friday evening. I'd love to. Is there a lady's locker room where I can change for dinner?"

"Of course. We will be dining at the club, so a business casual dress is required. No pants, suits, or trousers; see you later."

Sharply at 6:30, Hugh and the rest of his foursome were finishing their nine holes. Hugh begged off the drinks afterward as he saw Susan waiting outside the Pro shop. She was smiling as he walked up and instinctively wrapped an arm around her shoulder and said, "Glad you made it. I will be with you in just a second."

Hugh then walked inside and made arrangements with the Pro to allow him to take Susan out on the course to the 2nd and 3rd holes for a short lesson. Initially, he had thought about just taking her to the pitch and putt green but decided he didn't want to chance other people being around for her lesson.

Back outside, he held her hand and led her down to the golf cart, and they headed out.

"Are we really going to play golf? I don't think I am ready for that yet," Susan said in a somewhat worried but excited voice.

"You'll be fine. Trust me. We'll just practice some." Hugh said as he gave her back a soft pat.

When they got to the second hole and pulled up to the ladies' tee, Susan took in the beauty of the area. The sign said it was only a hundred yards to the green. Both sides of the fairway were lined with beautiful blooming azaleas, behind which were sparsely set pine trees.

"Why this looks like a picture postcard," Susan remarked as she got out of the golf cart and walked to the tee.

Hugh had never stopped to admire the landscape before, always intent on his next shot, but this time, Susan's remark caused him to stop and take in the beauty of their surroundings.

"It is pretty, isn't it? Do you remember your first lesson?"

"Yes, I think so. Head still. Eye on the ball. Only look after I finish my swing."

"Good. Let's give it a go then."

Hugh placed the ball on the tee, and Susan took her stance, doing everything correctly; however, the ball went sailing over the azaleas.

"Good for far, not for towards," Hugh remarked.

"What did I do wrong?"

"You forgot to aim. Lesson number 2."

Hugh showed her how to aim at the target, and on the next shot, the ball landed just off the edge of the green. Hugh was hoping for that because now he could get closer to her to show her how to pitch onto the green. He discussed the different clubs she could use to pitch with and suggested the seven iron. He showed her how to line up the ball from there, then came around behind her to show her how to place her hands on the club. He took a deep breath, moved by the smell of the perfume in her hair, and felt her tense. He decided it would be better if he instructed her from the side, so he stepped over to where the club and ball were between them and, using a different club, showed her how to pitch it.

Holding her tongue between her teeth as she concentrated, she hit the ball, and it went straight into the hole. Susan jumped up and down, raising the club in excited joy.

"I did it! I did it!" she shouted as she leaped into Hugh's arms and gave him a bear hug. "Did you see that?" she squealed.

"I certainly did," Hugh said as he took the opportunity to hug her again. "You take directions really well. Would you like to try another hole?"

"Absolutely! Lead on, oh wizard of the greens," Susan laughed as she trotted back to the golf cart.

The next hole was a par four with bunkers on both sides of the fairway and around the green. Susan's drive went into one of the fairway bunkers and necessitated a lesson on how to get out of a sand trap. As he watched her closely while she lined up her shot but instead of swinging her club, she slowly turned to him and whispered, "Look, a deer and her fawn."

Hugh turned his head to see the pair quietly walk across the green to partake of some of the azaleas. He had never given them much thought before, other than to shoo them off the course, but now he was seeing them through Susan's eyes and was just as mesmerized by their peacefulness. He walked over and stood beside Susan, who wrapped an arm around him.

"Aren't they beautiful?" she whispered.

The mother deer stopped her grazing and looked toward them. Then, without any sudden movements, she led her fawn into the woods.

"You know, I never really looked at them before. Thank you, Susan," Hugh whispered back.

Susan felt a warm glow fill her as she realized that she and Hugh were standing with one arm around each other.

She turned to Hugh, "I really like being here with you, Hugh."

"And I really like having you with me," Hugh replied and gave her a kiss on the cheek.

Susan blushed and said, "Are we still having a golf lesson?"

"Absolutely!" Hugh replied, and they continued to finish the hole with a putting lesson. Hugh took six balls, three for Susan and three for himself, placed them at varying distances from the hole. "Okay, whoever gets the most balls in the hole or closest wins a prize."

"Okay, you're on," Susan replied.

Susan was close with all three, but Hugh's first ball went in, and he said, "I win!"

"What did you win?" she asked.

"A kiss, of course! Pay up!"

Susan smiled. She had been waiting and hoping for this moment for some time. She reached up, gently cupping Hugh's face in her hands as she urged him down towards her and gave him a long, soft kiss. As she backed off, a little embarrassed by her own forwardness, Hugh pulled her back to him and kissed her again.

"You have enchanted me," he whispered. "Is there room in your heart for me?"

"I think there is a lot of room in my heart for you," she replied.

As they embraced again, more deer started coming out of the shadows, and Hugh commented that they were being watched. Susan turned to look and chuckled, "I think this place is enchanted. Do you think the enchantment you feel will fade when we leave the golf course?"

"Not a chance," Hugh replied. "But perhaps we should get back and turn in the golf cart. I am sure the guys in the shed are waiting for us." With that, they left.

Hugh barely remembered what he had for dinner that evening as he was too intent on what Susan had to say and how beautiful she looked as she talked comfortably with him over their meal. As he walked her to her car, they both felt the tension rise, and although Susan longed to invite him home with her, propriety made her stop short. Hugh opened her car door for her, and she turned to him. They both stammered over each other, trying to say goodnight, and Hugh laughed and said, "May I kiss you again?"

"Yes, please," was the only response before they were again in each other's arms.

Breathless, Susan slid out of his embrace and into her car.

"As much as I would love to ask you to come over, I feel like I should say that I will see you in the morning instead."

Hugh stuck his bottom lip out but said, "I suppose I understand, but I don't have to like it."

Susan gave a chuckle and blew him a kiss as he said he would have coffee ready for her in the morning.

Subsequently, when returning to Nellis AFB the next morning, Francois and Henri were pleasantly surprised to hear, "I have decided on a different plan for the two of you. We have training programs at several different Air Force bases in this country that could make good use of your talents. After working here in Nevada for two semesters, we will send you to different locations within the United States."

At that point, they both jumped up, grinning, shook his hand, and started filling out the application papers he had handed them.

 **CHAPTER THIRTY-THREE**

Another Postcard

Jane received another postcard and immediately called Kate.

"I got another postcard from Ward, this time from Paris! Listen to this! 'We arrived here in Paris but were very disappointed. We came here because Heather wanted to use a bidet, and they don't have any in our stalls.'"

Both Kate and Jane break out in laughter and can hardly stop.

"Is the handwriting the same?"

"No, it's entirely different. It is very dainty and looks like a lady wrote it."

"That's really funny. Do you think more than one person is doing this?"

"It must be because the other one was from London."

"I'll have to ask John what he thinks. You say this one is from Paris?"

"Yes, definitely. It even has a picture of the Eiffel Tower on the front."

"OK, keep in touch. Bye."

 # CHAPTER THIRTY-FOUR

Plan B Implemented

Having successfully heard all that was said in the Boss's first three meetings, which used the two mules plus several horses, the CIA agents in Paris were able to identify and follow the suicide bomber's trainers. They observed how they selected a trainee and who they were. They simply passed their information along to the FBI. One was arrested in New York before he could do any damage, another was arrested boarding a plane for the United States from Saudi Arabia, and the third was arrested after arriving in Miami from Paris.

Both Susan and Hugh were elated when they found that the two mules' listening devices were working so well. They called Tom immediately and agreed they would all get together for dinner to celebrate.

During the dinner, they discussed the danger of the Boss becoming suspicious and decided it would be necessary to implement Plan B.

The next time the Boss and his crew rented two mules and four horses to ride into their secret, remote location, two of the horses each had a listening device attached to a rear hoof with an antenna running up the back of its leg. After the meeting was well under way, one of the devices started to buzz.

"What is that noise?" yelled the Boss. "Where is it coming from?"

They found it was coming from the horse's hoof, grabbed it and its antenna, and yanked them off.

"There's our problem! No wonder our men got caught! Let's go back to the stable and find out who did this."

They returned to the rental stable and examined all the horses and mules' hooves, and found one more horse with a listening device installed.

All the employees of the stable pleaded innocence and went on to prove those were new horses recently obtained from the big horse auction. The transactions were in cash, as is normal, and no record was kept concerning the previous owners.

The Boss was furious. He decided to contact his leader and explain what happened. If someone is spying on his group using this method, they may be spying on others as well. This resulted in an order that before riding any animal, its hooves or feet must be carefully inspected for foreign objects, just like in the United States, where they inspect the shoes of everyone getting on an airplane.

When Hugh reported to the President that Plan B had been both devised and implemented and what the results were, he could hardly stop laughing.

 **CHAPTER THIRTY-FIVE**

Plan C

By mid-August, the hot summer days had turned into rainy ones, which, on this day, matched Susan's mood.

Susan walked into Hugh's office with a glum look on her face shaking her head and saying, "Our postcard system is falling apart. Jane got a postcard from Ward mailed in Helen, North Carolina." She took her raincoat off, shaking them both emphasizing her mood.

"Really, what did it say?" replied Hugh, leaning back in his chair, linking his fingers behind his head and trying not to grin as he suspected the answer.

"It said something about Ward seeing his cousin, Henry, a white horse, pulling a wagon full of tourists down the main street in Helen. Why are you smiling like that?" she asked, confused that he wasn't as mad as she was.

"I'm smiling because I was sure it would happen sooner or later. Kate's file showed she had a mischievous sense of humor, so I considered that once she heard about our postcards, she would talk other friends into joining in the fun," Hugh said as he got out of his chair to come closer to Susan.

Susan continued, shaking her head, and, with a heavy sigh, said, "It's even more complicated than that. Jane is convinced that all the postcards are coming from someone who knows her because her husband is named Henry."

"That's even better," said Hugh, "That means she doesn't suspect her friend, Kate, or Kate's husband, the FBI agent, of being involved. You see now how well Deep Cover works? The more of these extraneous postcards Jane gets, the better it will be. Susan nods slowly and says, "Is there anything we should do?"

"No," Hugh replied, "In fact, now that the CIA has the Boss's team under surveillance in England, Algeria, and France, we might as well back off and bring home the two mules before they get in trouble somehow. Their lease should not be renewed. Your agent in Las Vegas should be able to take care of that."

"Okay, I'll call him," she said as she got out her cell phone and started out of Hugh's office.

She was back in just a few minutes. She said to Hugh, "Our agent thinks that those two mules have done such an outstanding job keeping suicide bombers outside the United States that they should have some recognition."

"That sounds like a great idea! That should be fun! Maybe I can get the President to join us. I am having a meeting with him next week. I'll see what I can do. By the way, he said he would like to meet you, so you should come along with me."

Susan had never personally met the President and often wondered if she would ever be assigned to his detail. A White House assignment had always been her ultimate goal.

"Really? That's awesome. I would love to meet the President."

She thought to herself. *There I go again. Whenever I look at Hugh, I can't seem to carry on a conversation without inserting the word 'love' into it somewhere. I sound like a rookie.*

 # CHAPTER THIRTY-SIX

The President Meets Susan

The following week, sharply at 10 o'clock, Hugh and Susan left the CIA building for their 10:30 meeting with the President. After waiting a few minutes, they are ushered into his office. The President greeted them warmly and congratulated them on a job well done. He went on to say he could never have found two better people to do it.

Hugh told him about the FBI agent's suggestion to have a presentation ceremony honoring the two mules and thanking their owner. He advised The President their thought of doing this would be when the mules arrived at the Las Vegas airport on their way home and asked him if he would like to attend. The President said he would like that very much if it could be worked into his schedule. He instructed Hugh to keep in touch with his Chief of Staff on that subject.

"By the way," the President said, "What is the name of the owner of the mules?"

"John Smith," piped up Susan.

"Very good. I would like to meet him so I can thank him personally."

"I am sure he would like that very much," replied Susan

The President then said, "Now that I have you both here, I would like to hear about something else. You know I am a direct kind of guy, so all I want is some straightforward answers. Susan, I understand you have asked your boss if you could be transferred to the CIA, and he said no. Is that correct?"

Susan looked over at Hugh and said sheepishly, in a whisper, "Yes, sir, he said that I was too valuable to the FBI to waste my time working for the CIA."

The President, with his eyes darting back and forth between Susan and Hugh, waited a few seconds, then said to Hugh, "Don't you think, Hugh, that you could find a further need for Susan at the CIA as an FBI Liaison Agent?"

"Yes sir, yes sir, we need her to stay on with us. She is invaluable!" he replied.

The President, with a knowing smile, said quietly, "This meeting is over."

As they walked out the door, just before it closed, the President saw them take each other's hand and said to himself, "Those two are in love. I wonder how long it will take them to admit it."

He then called his secretary in to make a note to have Susan transferred to the White House FBI staff when this mission was over.

"Well, Susan, it looks like it is time for you to make some arrangements in Las Vegas," Hugh said.

"What do you mean?"

"Now that you have met the President, you need to introduce him to John Smith. I suggest you put your agent on to finding out when the mules will arrive there."

"Okay, you'll be going there with me, won't you?

"Oh no. That's inside the United States type work, not my jurisdiction, strictly the FBI."

"What do you think I should tell John Smith?"

"Nothing. The President will tell him all he wants him to know."

Susan got in touch with the agent in Las Vegas who had interviewed John Smith about leasing the mules to Francois and Henri and made arrangements to meet him at the airport when he brought his truck and trailer to pick up the two mules. John Smith advised he would be there a couple of days earlier than the plane with the mules in order to enjoy a visit to Las Vegas.

That's good news to them, so Susan passed along the available time frame to Hugh for the President's Chief of staff to work with.

 # CHAPTER THIRTY-SEVEN

The President's Visit

No part of the Las Vegas airport shaded any part of the tarmac, so Susan was glad that the FBI's SUV had blackout windows in addition to great air conditioning. Susan sat behind the steering wheel with John Smith next to her, and while waiting, Susan turned to John, "Why did you decide to lease these two mules instead of selling them?"

"Those two Frenchmen wanted to buy five mules. They said they had plenty of money, but I only have ten good mules, so it would be like selling my business. I don't own anything else. If I sold half of my mules, I wouldn't have a business. Besides, it is too big an effort and time to train new mules. Just breaking in a mule to ride is much harder than breaking in a horse. These mules have to be taught to let totally novice, and beginner riders ride them. I told them I could not sell them any of my mules because they have been trained for the dangerous trail they have to take. That's the easiest part because they are so smart and sure-footed. I could never teach a horse to ride that trail. But they begged so hard that out of the goodness of my heart, I agreed to lease them two, provided they pay upfront and pay for all their travel expenses. Now, tell me again why we are sitting here."

"I have been instructed not to tell you anything, but I will tell you this: there is a man coming in on a private plane who said he wanted to meet you and thank you. That's all I can say."

Just as she said that a large plane came in and touched down on the nearest runway, and the radio in the car crackled on with, "FBI number one, this is the tower. The field is open. You are cleared to drive to the plane that just landed."

Susan started the car, and off they went.

"That looks like Air Force One!" shouts John.

"It is. Hang on; we'll be there in a minute," Susan replied.

"You mean the Head of the FBI wants to meet me?" John asks.

Susan ignored the question and replied, "Just follow me."

They got out of the car, and Susan climbed the steps with John close behind. At the top, they were met by a gentleman who escorted them back to the President's office. He rose from his chair and came forward as Susan stepped aside, saying, "Mister President, I would like you to meet John Smith."

While he shook the President's hand, John was dumbfounded, trying hard to think of something to say.

He need not bother because the President took over the conversation.

"I know that this comes as a surprise. I just wanted to meet you and thank you and tell you that your mules, while they were overseas, performed a great service for the United States. Those few of us who know the details appreciate it and would like to continue to keep it as quiet as possible."

The President then turned to Susan and said, "Thank you, Susan. You did a great job. Goodbye and good luck."

With that, they left, got back in the car, and Susan said to John, "Wasn't that nice?"

John finally got his voice back, "Boy-oh-boy, am I glad I didn't sell those two mules!"

 # CHAPTER THIRTY-EIGHT

Love Proclaimed

After dropping John off at his truck, Susan headed back to her hotel. She ignored the radio, and the quiet brought thoughts of Hugh. Her mind began to have a conversation with itself. *It's too bad Hugh didn't come along on this trip. I wish he were here. This would be a great time for us to get to know each other better. I wonder what he is doing right now.*

When she walked into the lobby, she was astounded to see Hugh sitting there by the front door, waiting for her to come in. With a warm smile on her face, she exclaimed, "What are you doing here?"

"I missed you," he said, jumping up from his chair. "While you were gone, every time I walked into my office, I felt lonely. I simply couldn't stand your being so far away. This is a serious problem. We've got to do something about it."

Susan felt herself blush as she realized the impact of his heartfelt comment. She held his gaze with her eyes, put one hand gently on his cheek, and brushed her lips lightly against his.

"Maybe, here in Las Vegas, we can put our jobs aside and take a vacation," she said softly to him as she let her hand move from his cheek to his ear, to his neck, and come to rest on his collar bone. Her tender touch seared him like a hot iron, and he wrapped her in his arms, bringing his lips down to meet hers again.

They stand there with their arms around each other and their faces close enough to whisper.

"What is your room number?" she asks, almost inaudibly.

He freed one hand, reached in his side coat pocket, and pulled out a key.

"Seven thirty, here is a second key," he said, his voice husky with passion.

She took the key and whispered, "I'll pack and check out."

He whispered, "I'll be waiting for you."

He was standing in his room by the door when she tapped on it. He opened the door, and she rushed in. As soon as she put down her suitcase, they embraced each other.

There was very little conversation for the next two days and nights. It was what you might call a "pre-wedding honeymoon." Various meals were ordered via room service. Between passionate lovemaking sessions, they revealed thoughts and feelings they had harbored toward each other. They shared pivotal moments from their past and dreams of the future.

A few things were said, like, "My mother will like you very much." and, "I am sure my children will love you." But that was as close as either would venture to the three-word sentence that rings of permanence.

Finally, Susan says, "I think it's Monday. Isn't it time that we get back to work?"

"No," Hugh replied, "this assignment has been successfully completed, and we both have been directed to take two-week vacations. I was hoping we could find somewhere we could go together."

"How lovely; I can suggest the perfect place to go," she said as she rolls over on top of him, propping herself up on top of his chest, "Charleston, South Carolina. It is a beautiful city. You'll love it, and you will get to meet my mother who lives there."

Hugh nodded vigorously, "That's definitely something I need to do, and the sooner, the better, but first..." his sentence trailed off as he grabbed her and flipped them both so that he was laying on top of her.

"I have other more enticing business to attend to."

He pulled the covers over his head and snuggled down into her as she giggled and gasped with pleasure.

 # CHAPTER THIRTY-NINE

Charleston

After talking it over carefully, they decided to take their return flights back to D.C. and make the trip to Charleston in Hugh's car since it was an easy one-day drive and it would be much more convenient to have his car when they got there.

Driving over the huge Cooper River bridge gave Hugh a nice panoramic view of the city, which he appreciated and admired. They continued on Route 17 through Charleston across the less impressive Ashley River Bridge to James Island, where Susan's mother, Betty O'Connor, lived.

Susan had been talking to her mother while Hugh drove to keep her abreast of their progress. When they pulled up to her house, she was already coming out the front door to greet them.

There were hugs all around while Susan introduced her mother to Hugh. Hugh still had his arm around Susan as they walked into the house.

They sat down in the living room, but it was obvious from the view of the dining room that Betty had already prepared dinner for the three of them.

"Susan has told me so much about you that I laid in some Jack Daniels and some Beefeater's gin. How about a martini before dinner, or would you prefer a shot or two of whiskey?" Betty asked, excited to finally meet him.

As she walked over to the sideboard, they both eagerly answered together, "Jack over ice would be fine."

During the ensuing conversation, Hugh ventured a question to Betty, "Did Bob ask permission of your father before he proposed marriage to you?"

"Yes, he did," she replied," but only after I persuaded him to. Bob had been a Marine Colonel and told me he had never heard a Marine Colonel ask permission to do anything. He said it was always act first and discuss later."

Susan was elated that her mom and Hugh were getting along so well together. She excused herself, got up from the dinner table, and proceeded to the restroom, feeling a little light-headed from the alcohol and the tenor of the conversation. In such a fine old southern home, Hugh felt compelled to stand as Susan left the room.

As he sat back down, Hugh continued, "Well, I may be a little old-fashioned, but it seems to me to be the right thing to do. Now that Susan has left the room, may I have your permission to ask her to marry me?"

"As I said before, Susan has told me so much about you that I feel like I know you already. Even if I didn't, I trust my daughter completely and am sure she knows what she is doing," she smiled at Hugh, and he noticed her eyes get a little misty. "If Bob were here, I am sure he would be delighted to have you for a son-in-law," she dabbed her napkin at the corner of her eyes.

"I have another question," Hugh said. "I would like to find someplace romantic here in Charleston to take Susan to and propose. Do you know of any place that would be suitable?"

Betty thought about that for a little while. Then she said, "It's been a long time since I thought about it, but I would say the Battery would be the place. That's where Bob proposed to me."

"The Battery? Where is that, and why is it called the Battery? That doesn't sound very romantic to me."

Betty laughed. "No, it doesn't, does it. The Battery is down at the southern tip of Charleston. That's where the two rivers, the Cooper and the Ashley, come together and form the harbor. There is a park there called White Point Gardens with a number of antique cannons that children play on. I guess that's why they call it The Battery. It is really a beautiful park with large trees and a gazebo in the middle."

Hugh shook his head. "So far, nothing sounds romantic to me."

Betty smiled. "That's true. It only becomes romantic at night when the teenagers, who have been to a movie or dance and have only recently gotten their driver's licenses, bring their parent's car with their date and probably another couple with them and park next to the sea wall for a little innocent kissing and whispering. It's dark and quiet, and nobody bothers them."

Hugh nodded in understanding and teasingly whispered, "It sure sounds like you are speaking from experience. How many times have you been there?"

Betty sat back and looked at the ceiling. In a deeply southern accent, she drawled, "A gentleman never asks a lady such things!"

Hugh turned very serious now and said, "You had better give me some directions on how to get there."

Betty chuckled and said, "You need not worry about that. Just mention to Susan when you are in the car that you would like to drive by the Battery. She'll get you there."

The next day Susan took Hugh on a little tour of Charleston. They went down to the Meeting Street market and looked through the shops, took the horse

& buggy tour down East Bay Street past Rainbow Row, around the Battery, looked at the beautifully restored old homes, and learned a little about the history of Charleston. On the way back, they had the driver stop at Adger's Wharf and walked down the quaint narrow cobblestone lane to Susan's favorite seafood restaurant perched along the water. Cold beer and oysters were perfect for lunch on this hot summer day.

They strolled back to the car, looking in shop windows as they walked hand in hand, enjoying each other's company.

The following day Betty invited them to join her at her beach house on Folly Beach. Hugh was surprised and delighted to see that the beach held only one motel and quaint shops and eateries on only one street. The rest of the island held private homes. He took Betty and Susan out to eat at a restaurant that had live entertainment. After a few drinks and some coaxing, since it was open mic night, he borrowed a guitar and played a couple of Jimmy Buffet tunes to the delight of everyone.

Betty's beach house was exactly as Hugh had imagined. It was an old Colonial style, made of wood and painted white with teal trim and a teakwood door. They walked up the side steps to the second floor to enter the house. The main room was a large kitchen-diner with appliances that looked as though they had been there since the 1950s. There was a short wide refrigerator which Betty referred to as the icebox and a gas stove oven. The dining table and chairs were painted wood. Beyond the kitchen was a large, square room that held several couches and chairs, all covered with drop cloths which Betty instructed Hugh and Susan to take off and put away in the cedar chest. There are two doors on each side of this room, each opening into a bedroom. The one bathroom off the dining room held an old claw-footed bathtub.

Hugh decided that his favorite room was on the other side of the back door upstairs as it opened onto a screened porch that overlooked the ocean. An old wooden swing hung from the rafters, and several comfortable wicker chairs were strategically placed to enjoy the view.

There did not seem to be an entrance to the first floor without going outside. Betty explained that she inherited the house and that originally the upstairs was the servants' quarters, but she liked the view better, so she put a kitchen downstairs and rented that part of the house out during the tourist season.

The next morning Susan, Hugh, and Betty, were enjoying a breakfast of eggs, bacon, and grits together when Hugh turned to Betty and said, "I understand you know some interesting stories about Charleston."

"I suppose I do. Let me clean up the dishes a bit while you and Susan enjoy the morning air on the porch, and I'll join you with some fresh coffee."

It felt good to breathe in the sweet, salty ocean air, and when Betty came out, Hugh asked her again for some stories. She set the tray of coffee down, and as she started to pour each of them a cup, she said, "One that comes to mind is about the propeller club. But you should really find a man to tell you the full story because it was and still is a club of men only. I don't know if it still has meetings, but I can tell you what little I know."

"Have you ever met a harbor pilot?" she asked.

"No, I can't say that I have. Do you mean the man who meets the ship out in the channel and brings it into the dock? Have you met one?" he replied.

"Yes. It is a tough job because he must have intimate knowledge about everything in the harbor, particularly the tides and their effect on the currents.

He must be on call all day and all night for obvious reasons. As such, he almost always passes his job down to his son, and no one else gets an opportunity for it."

"So, is that how the propeller club was formed?"

"I suppose it must have been because that is one of their unique requirements. To join, you have to be the son of one of the members."

"Really? What else do you know about it?"

"The only meeting I know about them having is an annual dinner meeting they have a few days before Christmas. They all get dressed in tuxedos and go to dinner in a private dining room in one of the downtown hotels. I heard two things about it— that it included many of the most prominent men in Charleston and that it was an excellent dinner that included two cigars at each place setting. It sounded odd to me, but, as I said, you need to find a man to tell you more about it."

"I guess you are right. It does sound unique. I imagine Charleston must have been quite a different place when you were a little girl."

"It was. Nothing like today. I can remember one incident at the annual Christmas Ball held in the Hibernian Hall. All the young couples who liked to dance would go, some married and some unmarried. One year there was a big scandal when, about a week before the ball, it was discovered that one of the ladies expected to attend was a divorced woman. Divorce was very rare back then and usually involved infidelity on the woman's part, which was quite scandalous. Many people were shocked! Several ladies said that if a divorced woman would be there, they were not going, period. I can't remember any of the details, but I think in the end, they all, or almost all, went to the ball anyway because they were very curious to see her."

"Well, that's certainly a far cry from any thinking on that subject today!"

"Yes, things were different then. A lady would not even think of going to church on Sunday without wearing a hat and white gloves. And you would buy groceries by calling a local store and having them delivered and only pay for them once a month. Maybe we are getting back to something like that. I hope so."

Betty finished her coffee and said, "Enough reminiscing now. It's a lovely morning, so why don't the two of you take a stroll down the beach."

"Great idea," Susan said, getting up and reaching out her hand to Hugh. "Come on, let's see if we can discover some beautiful shells to take back with us."

They didn't find any shells but realized they had walked all the way to the pier, so they headed up to the small arcade and then crossed the street to peruse the gift shops.

Two days later, they were back in town at Betty's home. Hugh had said he needed to pick up something and would be back shortly. Betty told him to be back before five as she would not hold supper for anyone. Susan told him to pick up some ice cream on the way home as she was making a pecan pie for tonight's dessert and preferred hers a la mode. Betty was busy heading shrimp for her low country boil and had enlisted Susan to shuck corn and wash new potatoes.

After dinner, with the dishes put away and the kitchen wiped down, Betty settled into her study with a good book. Hugh took Susan by the hand and asked her to come sit with him on the porch swing. It was a nice breezy evening, and within a few minutes, a light rain began to fall. Hugh put his arm around Susan as she put her feet up on the side of the swing and snuggled into him. As he rocked the swing with the rhythm of the rain, he said, "Will you marry me?"

She sat up and looked at him. Before she could say anything, he pulled a small ring box out of his pocket and gave it to her. Before opening it, she said, "I thought you'd never ask. I'd love to marry you, but I'd like to make sure that's alright with your kids first."

They talked it over for quite a while and decided the best way to inform them would be to get hotel and plane reservations for them and invite them to Charleston, saying they would have some important news when they got here.

 **CHAPTER FORTY**

Orlando

When the wedding announcement and invitation reached the President's secretary, she immediately sent word to Susan's FBI boss that Susan would be transferred to the White House FBI contingent in accordance with his earlier instructions.

It was a small church wedding. Tom was there together with several of Hugh's friends at the CIA and Hugh's three children. The President sent his best wishes. Betty was impressed. She invited the three children to spend a week with her. She found that they already knew many games to play, so she took them to Folly Beach and taught them how to take a net on a long pole down to the surf and catch blue crabs. They all had a great time together.

Susan and Hugh left in his car, bound for Orlando to spend their honeymoon. They headed south on Route 17, stopping the first night in Savannah, then Saint Augustine, then Orlando.

At breakfast, Susan turned to Hugh and said, "There is a place here, near Orlando, that I think you would enjoy visiting. Do you know who John Wycliffe was?"

"John Wycliffe, it seems like I know that name. Didn't he have something to do with the Bible?"

"Yes, he lived in England in the 1300s. He was a theologian, philosopher, and church reformer. He argued that Scripture was the primary basis for

Christianity and promoted the first complete translation of the Bible into English."

"Wow, that was long before printing presses. They must have done that by writing on scrolls."

Susan chuckled. "Probably, anyway, I thought you would be interested since you are always trying to find ways to prevent wars through education. There is a place here called Wycliffe which is helping people around the world translate the Bible into their language."

"Really? That's an awfully big ambition. How did they ever get started?"

"I thought you'd never ask," she kidded him, "Let me read you this piece of their history." Susan looked on her cell phone and read, "In 1917, a missionary named William Cameron Townsend (nicknamed Cam) traveled to Guatemala and sold Spanish Bibles. However, he was shocked that many people couldn't read the language in the books. Instead, they spoke Cakchiquel, an indigenous language that did not have a translated version of the Bible. Townsend believed everyone should be able to understand the Bible, so he started the Summer Institute of Linguistics (SIL), which trained people to translate the Bible. In 1942, Townsend officially founded Wycliffe Bible Translators. In the year 2000, they completed their 500th translation, and Wycliffe adopted a new challenge; a goal of seeing a Bible translation project started in every language still needing one by 2025. Lately, they have decided to push that goal back to 2050."

Hugh was amazed at her research.

"How did you know all about this?" he asked.

"Well, when you originally told me about your college of religion idea, I got curious about just how widespread Christianity actually was and started googling information in my spare time. I stumbled on this in my web search and was just fascinated."

"I knew from the start that you were more than just a pretty face," he teased. While driving down to visit the Wycliffe Bible Translators, a small smile appeared on Hugh's face. Susan noticed and said, "I can see you are smiling, Hugh. What are you thinking about?"

"I was just thinking about a dumb idea I had several years ago."

"A dumb idea? I find that hard to believe. What was it?"

"The idea? Well, it was a plan to improve the world if I could get it funded. Using the Gospel according to John, which is the shortest of the four gospels, I would print thousands, or maybe millions, of copies and simply fly over non-Christian countries and drop them, depending on the power of the story to do the work without the need for preaching or teaching."

"That doesn't seem so dumb to me."

"The dumb part is that I didn't even consider the language barrier."

"Oh, I see what you mean."

In order to reach the Wycliffe Translators south of Orlando, the route first took them east on Curry Ford Road, which turned out to be almost a small town in itself. It had the new, modern five-lane main street with the center lane used primarily for stopping and turning in and out of parking lots or supplying a second left-turn lane at intersections. Because of the convenience, every kind of shop could be found, many restaurants with Italian, Vietnamese, Chinese, and Korean cuisine, plus shoe and watch repair shops, beauty shops, drugstores, hardware stores, and practically everything. Beyond that, the drive became fairly monotonous, affording them time to discuss their future plans.

Hugh mentioned that the President had told him he was being considered for promotion to Department

Head of a new effort the CIA was considering. Since the overall purpose of the CIA was to influence foreign governments to adopt democratic principles, the recent virus pandemic had suggested a new approach to the problem. A helpful approach to solving internal national problems could prove much more effective than anything else.

Hugh was very enthusiastic and even suggested a name for it; The Mercy Department.

The President had told Hugh to think about the details of how it would be implemented, and they would discuss it at length whenever he was ready.

Hugh had set the address of the Wycliffe Translators into his GPS, which showed them to just continue East on Curry Ford Road for several miles until they turned right onto the ramp leading to route 417 going South. When instructed, they exited 417 and continued toward the East for a few miles when Hugh suddenly stopped.

"What's the matter?" asked Susan.

"Look at the GPS." Said Hugh, pointing at it. "It's showing no streets or roads. It thinks we are out in a field somewhere."

"How odd," he said as he made a U-turn. There were no other cars around anywhere.

Susan pointed out to the right, saying, "There is a lady walking her dog. Let's ask her for directions," as she rolled down her window.

"Excuse me, can you tell us how to find a street called Translation Way?"

The lady stopped and pulled out her cell phone and punched it a few times, and said, "You need to go back that way, cross the railroad tracks and turn left." She said, smiling. Apparently, it wasn't the first time she had to help with directions.

As they continued back the way they had come, Hugh remarked, "I don't remember crossing any railroad tracks. However, there are some off to the left, there, paralleling our road. Let's turn left at this stoplight and cross them and see what happens."

Sure enough, as soon as they crossed the railroad tracks, the GPS picked up again with the announcement, "Turn left."

They both just looked at each other and grinned.

The further they drove, the quieter and more deep-in thought Hugh became.

"Just think of how tough the language barrier is," he said. "Not only do you have to find people with dual language capability, but you also have to recruit, from that small number, enthusiastic people. That must be close to an insurmountable problem."

"There it is! See the sign? Wycliffe Associates," she exclaimed.

In addition to finding many different language Bibles they could buy, even one written Gullah. This impressed Susan as Gullah was often spoken by native Charlestonians and others living in the low country of South Carolina. They also found that the people doing the translating were mostly natives living in different countries, sometimes subject to antagonistic governments. The humanitarianism in Hugh was piqued by this information.

Hugh insisted on meeting with the man in charge. He explained who he was and what he did and ended with, "As a response to the Pandemic which resulted in the indiscriminate deaths of many of both our allies and enemies, the CIA has formed a new division, called the Mercy Division. It is expected to produce major international cooperation. Your people, scattered throughout the world, should be ideal recruits for our Mercy Division. If you supply me with the names of those people, I will see what I can do to help them."

Susan frowning, pulled Hugh aside, "Surely you realize these people will be in great danger if someone finds out the CIA is involved with what they are doing."

Hugh replied, "Of course, that's why they will all have to be kept under Deep Cover."

 **CHAPTER FORTY-ONE**

The Grand Canyon

As they were driving away from Wycliffe Associates, Susan turned to Hugh and said, "You know, your children have been so understanding about me. I think when we get back to Charleston, we should do something nice for them."

"What did you have in mind?" Hugh asked.

"When I was talking to them, I asked what they liked to do most, and all three said that they liked to fly, but they very seldom had a chance to take a trip. So, I thought it would be a nice trip to fly out west and visit the Grand Canyon. I've never been there, and Tom said there was an airport very near the canyon in a little town called Tusayan in Arizona. That's where John Smith has his mules," Susan replied.

"That's a great idea! I wouldn't mind seeing those mules myself. Let's do it."

When they got back to Charleston and told the children about their plans, they were delighted.

"You'll also get to meet a real cowboy. His name is John Smith, and he owns a small herd of mules that take riders down into the Grand Canyon," Susan explains. "I am sure your dad will enjoy meeting him too."

 # CHAPTER FORTY-TWO

Jacob Cohen comes to America

Earlier, when Francois and Henri proposed and assured Ruth and Eve that they had sufficient funds for the first year while they found a job, Ruth and Eve proceeded with their plans for a double wedding. Ruth let her father know that they are setting a date for two weeks from now.

Jacob Cohen called his travel agent in Paris and informed her that he needed to be in Las Vegas, Nevada, in two weeks but must travel via Lakeland, Florida, where he would want to spend a few days before going on to Las Vegas. He requested a flight into either Tampa or Orlando, a rental car for the round trip to Lakeland, and reminded her he would like to travel first class. He also requested she confirms reservations for him at a Bed and Breakfast in Lakeland. Apologizing for all the requests, he explained to her that he was going there to see the buildings designed by Frank Lloyd Wright. Becoming somewhat tense as he realized that this whirlwind romance was actually culminating in marriage to a man he had not yet met, he paced the floor trying to sort out his feelings until the phone rang.

The travel agent reported that there were no flights from Paris to Tampa or Orlando, and he must travel through Atlanta, Georgia. She remembered some joke about traveling through Atlanta about whether you are going to either heaven or hell; you have to go through Atlanta and relayed that to Jacob to appease his frustration. She also found that there are many nice places to eat in Lakeland, but when she requested bed and breakfast, her search engine simply listed hotels and motels that offer breakfast which was practically all of them. She didn't know what that request was all about, so the next day, she called him back.

She explained to him that all the hotels and motels in Lakeland apparently include breakfast in their price for renting a room and didn't quite understand his special request for a Bed and Breakfast.

He explained to her that his two daughters had been touring the United States for two reasons; to visit places designed by Frank Lloyd Wright and to meet Americans and get to know what it is like to live there.

They had found that the easiest way to meet people was by staying at bed and breakfasts. They were private homes that have been converted into small inns which rent a few rooms, usually less than a dozen, and provide a communal breakfast at a single large table.

She said, "Oh, I quite understand now. That does sound like a lot of fun. I would like to do that myself. I'll get right on it."

The next day she called him again and told him about flying through Atlanta, Georgia, and changing planes to Tampa, Florida. She said she had found him a nice bed and breakfast home on a lake in Lakeland that she was sure he would enjoy.

Looking forward to all of the adventures ahead of him, Jacob Cohen boarded the Delta Airlines flight in Paris with mixed emotions. Ahead of him on the line boarding, the same plane was a young lady who reminded him of his deceased wife. She looked just like that beautiful movie star and famous inventor Hedy Lamarr as had his deceased wife when she was younger. He couldn't help but be reminded that they had often planned to go to the United States on vacation but never got around to it.

 # CHAPTER FORTY-THREE

Camille

When he got into his seat and fastened his seatbelt, he adjusted his pillow, knowing that as soon as he heard the noise of the engines running, he would feel drowsy and may even go to sleep before they got off the ground. He was always a relaxed, comfortable passenger.

He slept soundly through most of the flight dreaming about someone who looked like Hedy Lamarr. Finally, when the announcement came that they were about to land in New York, he woke and had to think for a minute to get his bearings again. He had to wait two hours for his flight to Atlanta and decided to get a local newspaper to pass the time by learning what was currently going on in America and also brush up on his English.

After buying a paper and finding his departure gate at the airport, he settled into the waiting area only to be surprised to see that an attractive young lady was doing the same thing, reading a newspaper and apparently waiting for the same plane. She looked up, and he nodded to her and smiled, searching his brain for some excuse he could use to introduce himself. He gave up and went back to his own newspaper.

When they boarded the plane, he was disappointed to see she was not seated in the first-class section where he was. However, in Atlanta, it was a completely different story. The plane to Tampa was smaller and all one class of seating. To his delight, he found himself sitting next to her in the waiting area.

She turned to him and said, "Are you from Tampa?"

"No, I am not," he replied in French, thinking maybe this would impress her.

"Oh, too bad," she said, "I was looking for someone to help me out."

"What kind of help do you need?" he asked, thinking this is just the opening I need.

"I'm trying to find out if there is a train or bus I can take to get from Tampa to Lakeland. It can't be too far. There must be something available. I've even asked people who live in Tampa. They don't seem to know either."

Jacob smiled. "What an amazing coincidence! I am going to Lakeland and have a rental car reserved. I can take you wherever you want to go. Anyway, there is probably not any train or bus. The United States is so large they tell me that owning a car is almost a necessity just to go to the grocery store."

"Really! I am sorry to hear that. Maybe I made a mistake coming here. My name is Camille," she said, putting out her hand.

"I am Jacob Cohen," he said, taking her hand. "By the way, why did you come here?"

"It's a long story. When I was in college, I majored in Psychology, particularly the psychology of marketing. But I never worked at it. I got married instead. When my husband passed away, I decided I should go back to school, graduate school, in fact, to learn enough to support myself. One of the courses was to study the psychology of someone highly successful in their field. It's amazing how many of those commit suicide. Anyway, I chose to study Frank Lloyd Wright, partly because it would give me the excuse to visit the United

States. So, here I am, headed to Lakeland where he was commissioned to design a whole college."

"You cannot believe what a coincidence that is. As an architect, I am here because I have recently won a big contract largely because of my devotion to the type of architecture that Frank Lloyd Wright represents. This part of my trip is a detour suggested by my two daughters while I am actually traveling from Paris to Las Vegas to attend their double-wedding marriage ceremony. They wanted me to also see that college," Jacob explained.

Camille grinned as she said, "So, we are both going to the same place! But why aren't they getting married in France?"

He explained to her that he had been commissioned to design and build for clients here in America and had sent Ruth and Eve here to open a branch office for him. He explained that his daughter, Ruth, suggested he would enjoy visiting Lakeland on the way.

Camille said, "What a wonderful coincidence! My hobby is architecture, and I have hundreds of photos to prove it. It's too bad we didn't meet earlier. Is your wife waiting for you in Las Vegas?"

"No, I'm a widower," Jacob replied. "Unfortunately, I had often promised my wife that I would bring her on a trip to America, but we always seemed too busy to make it."

There was a short silence before Camille said, "I would love to meet your daughters before the double wedding. Since their mother won't be there, maybe I could go on to Las Vegas with you and be of some help."

Jacob was somewhat taken aback by her boldness. But a Frenchman never turns down the company of a beautiful woman, especially when it is so eagerly given.

"That's very sweet of you to suggest, and I would love to have you continue with me. However, they are both quite efficient and independent. I am sure they have every detail planned by now. The best thing you could do is to give me some support because I have never met either of these two men they are intent on marrying."

He was so happy she had volunteered on continued travel with him that he could barely stifle a big grin that kept creeping up to his lips.

At the Tampa airport, they went together to the rental car agency where his car had been reserved, and he offered to have them both sign the contract so she could drive the car too. As soon as they got in the car, Jacob took out his GPS, wet the suction cup, and installed it on the left upper corner of the windshield.

"This will take us where we are going and do it in French. Isn't that neat?" he said.

"I am here in America, and I am glad I speak French. That's even neater!" she said, smiling.

"I'm delighted to hear that. Where are you staying?"

"I don't know. I just got here and haven't found a place yet."

"The place where I am staying is so close that we could walk to the University to take the tour. Why don't we go by and see if they have a room available for you?"

"That would be nice," she replied warmly.

On the way, they started planning their trip to Las Vegas, including various options to propose to the airline that would enable them to fly together. As it happened, to their delight, there was another room available at the bed and breakfast in Lakeland. She also had no trouble booking a room in Las Vegas.

At dinner that night, Camille again asked why Las Vegas instead of France or anywhere else in the United States.

Jacob explained that he had sent them there to open a branch office for his architectural firm because he had a large contract to build a college there called a University of Religion. He went on to explain that a group of very rich French philanthropists had come up with the idea that religious wars could be ended by educating religious people on the details of other religions than theirs. The result would make them more tolerant of other religions because of their similarity. "For instance," he explained, "Very few Jewish people know that the person most cited in the Koran is their hero, Moses, and vice versa for the Muslims and the Old Testament. The United States is known for its tolerance of religious freedom, and one of its philanthropists owned a suitable piece of land near Las Vegas. They thought it would be the ideal place to build such a university for various reasons, including the liberal state laws there."

As he finished his explanation, he noticed Camille slowly shaking her head.

"It's a very noble thought and an excellent objective, but it'll never work. It's too impractical," she said.

"Really?" he countered. "What makes you say that?"

"Because you'll never find enough students to enroll in such an endeavor," she replied. "You'll have to find some alternative way to attract students."

"Well, I have been very concerned about that. Would you have any suggestions?" he asked.

"Yes, I would. I think I know how to solve that problem. I have been thinking about it while you were talking. The first thing you would have to do would be to change the name of the university. You will never get enough students if they think they are signing up to study religion. My suggestion would be a University of Foreign Languages. That way, you could easily work in courses about various countries' local customs, including its predominant religion. In addition, you might find that you can attract foreign language teachers to move to Las Vegas while continuing their career at which they are experts," she replied.

"Those are excellent ideas! How did I ever get this far without you? Where have you been all my life?" Jacob exclaimed.

Camille smiled shyly and said, "I'm starting to ask myself the same question."

They spent the next two days and nights having all their meals together and visiting the buildings of the college. By the second day, they were walking together, hand in hand.

Jacob had become enamored with his new friend. However, as he was packing for the next leg of their journey, doubt crept in like a little devil on his shoulder whispering in his ear. *"What are you doing? She is much too young for you. I can hear Ruth saying, "You're robbing the cradle, dad!" And she would have a point.*

Camille was also having some anxiety over this next adventure as the conversation played in her head. *I hope his daughters like me. I am sure he thinks he is too old for me, but I'll bet I could show him otherwise if I had half a chance.*

As they got seated on the plane, a direct flight from Tampa to Las Vegas, Jacob turned to Camille and said, "I hope you don't mind, but flying makes me sleepy. I'll probably sleep through most of the flight."

"No, I don't mind at all. Just hold my hand while we take off, please. Flying makes me anxious."

As soon as she squeezed his hand, he knew he would not be sleeping on this flight.

"So, tell me about yourself," he said, "How long do you expect to be in the United States?"

She said that she had originally planned to stay a week to do some sightseeing, but then she needed to get back home and start looking for a job. She said that she hoped to finish graduate school and get a job as a teacher; otherwise, her skills were pretty much confined to being a secretary.

Jacob didn't reply to all of that. Instead, he just nodded as he was deep in thought.

Camille said, "What's the matter? You seem suddenly distant."

"I'm just thinking hard about what I can say to you to persuade you to stay here with me."

She sat upright in her seat and turned to him with hopeful eyes, "That's easy. All you have to do is offer me a job."

"Done!" he said. "I am badly in need of a private secretary. When we get to Las Vegas, I will introduce you to everyone as my private secretary, newly hired. I will explain to everyone our new plan for the university, including its new name, and give you full credit." He was excited and wide awake now, going over in his mind the various conversations that must take place."

"Slow down," she said, "don't you think you should wait until your daughters meet me?"

"My daughters don't have to approve my choice of secretary."

"How about your group of philanthropists; will they go along with changing the name and direction?"

"Let me tell you about them. They are nine men, and seven of them have wives. The two single men are about your age, having recently made millions in the United States stock market. I am sure they have all been invited to the wedding, but I doubt if more than one or two will show up. They are all so taken up with running their own businesses that, except for selecting the site, they only seem interested in throwing money at the university project. It will be up to you and me and my daughter, Eve, who has a Master's in Business Administration, to spend it wisely."

"Well, my business skills are very limited. I'll have to leave that to you two. Do you have any specific duties you want me to perform? You must have a secretary back in France."

"Yes, I have. She has been with me for over ten years and is fully capable of running my office when I am away. After all, it is just a matter of keeping my architects busy and happy and fully supplied with whatever they need. Since revising the name and direction of the university was your idea, you will be responsible for publicity at the beginning and for recruitment of the language professors when we get it built. And, by the way, I will pay you three-quarters of the salary of my secretary in France, so you will have a raise to look forward to."

Camille was smiling contentedly through this whole conversation when suddenly she had a new thought and frowned.

Jacob noticed and said, "What's the matter with that?"

"Nothing. Nothing at all. It just occurred to me that your two daughters will be very surprised to meet me."

Laughing, Jacob replied, "What will surprise them is how much you look like pictures of their mother when she was a young girl."

"Please tell me more about your two daughters. Are they both about the same age?"

"They are the same age. Ruth is my biological daughter, and Eve is adopted. They grew up together, almost like twins, because we adopted Eve when they were both two years old. Her father was my partner when both her parents were killed in an automobile accident. I encouraged Ruth to study architecture and Eve to go to business school so they could both work for me when they were ready. So far, everything has worked out fine. However, I have a lot of doubts about this sudden double-wedding ceremony with two men I haven't met. They sound good over the phone; that's all I can say."

Camille took his hand and squeezed it.

"Let's have faith," she said.

 # CHAPTER FORTY-FOUR

The Meeting

When they got off the plane after landing in Las Vegas, Ruth and Eve were there to meet them. Jacob had told them a little about Camille on the phone, so they were anxiously looking forward to meeting her because they always had worried about him living alone ever since their mother had passed away. As soon as they saw her, both recognized how closely she resembled what a young version of their mother must have looked like.

"So, this is Camille. She's beautiful! I can see why you like her so much," said Ruth.

"Well, there is a lot more than beauty there. She is a very smart lady too," replied Jacob.

"I am very happy to meet you both," said Camille.

Jacob turned to Ruth and said, "Where are the two grooms? I seem to be surrounded by ladies."

"They are out at Nellis Air Force Base, either working at their new jobs or telling their boss they decided not to take it. Their boss seems delighted to have professors that can teach both French and Arabic to a selected group of Air Force personnel. He told them that he could help them with becoming United States citizens."

Turning to Camille, Jacob said, "Did you hear that, Camille?"

She had been standing right next to him, so the question was unnecessary. In fact, she had not strayed more than three feet from him ever since they got off the plane.

Camille was smiling as Jacob went on to say, "We are going to have two foreign language professors right here in our family. It should make your publicity job very easy."

Eve's eyebrows shot up as she said, "Is Camille going to be working with us?"

"Yes, she will start as my private secretary and will be responsible for publicity. Aside from you two, she is the smartest girl I have ever met. It was her idea to change the name of the university to make it possible to attract student enrollment which I heartily endorse and have yet to explain to our philanthropists. But let's talk about the wedding if you are so sure there is going to be one. Frankly, I am not yet convinced."

A look of confusion and dismay came over Ruth and Eve. They slowly turned toward each other and mouthed, "What!"

There was a long moment of silence as the tension started to build in them,

Ruth recovered first and, with a sigh, said, "Dad, you will meet them both as soon as we get back to the hotel. I am sure you will find they are both perfect gentlemen and worthy of your trust."

They all return quietly to the hotel to find Francois and Henri were standing there at the front door waiting for them. Ruth introduced them to her dad, and he immediately invited them to come up to his room. He turned to Ruth and Eve and said, "will you excuse us, please? We will call you in time for dinner."

Ruth nodded, "Of course." She turned to Camille and said, "Come with us, Camille. We've got a lot to talk about."

Jacob, Francois, and Henri got on the elevator together, and before the door was closed, Jacob said,

"Those two girls are all the family I've got left, you know."

"Yes, sir, we realize that," said Francois. "We have no intention of taking them anywhere. We are working hard to find jobs, become citizens, and live here in Las Vegas."

Jacob simply nodded and kept quiet until they reached his room. They stood quietly and waited while he tipped the bellhop and invited them to take a seat on the couch. He sat down opposite them, leaned forward, and said, "All right, tell me all about yourselves. Why did you come to the United States?"

"Before we answer that, we need to explain how much our life has changed since we came here. In addition to falling in love with your two daughters, we have also fallen in love with the United States," Francois explained.

"Really? You have fallen in love with this country? How so?" Jacob asked, pulling his head back with a confused frown."

"Our first experience was one of freedom. We had been told that the different states had different laws, and yet when we drove across a state line, there was no necessity to show our passports or identification. There was just a sign that said 'Welcome.' We were amazed," said Francois.

"Yes, sir, that is true, and what we will be telling you is what they call a confession in the Catholic Orphanage where we were brought up until the age of five," adds Henri.

Jacob sat back to get more comfortable and said, "I'm all ears."

Francois continued, "Although it was a Catholic Orphanage. We were adopted by a wealthy Muslim family on the promise that they would put us through college. The family had several daughters but only one son, a couple of years older than us, who we were required to call the Boss. When his father was killed in a battle, he went berserk, developing a deep hatred for Israel and its allies, including the United States. He even started finding evil ways to get revenge. He sent us here on a mission to acquire mules to use for his secret, secluded meetings. We were told to act like tourists but avoid being photographed and not to try to get in touch with him unless absolutely necessary."

Jacob did not like this information but decided to remain open-minded.

"But how did you meet Ruth and Eve?" Jacob asked.

"When they got on our plane in New York speaking French, we struck up an acquaintance," Francois replied.

"For some time, I thought they were FBI agents following us." Henri volunteered, smiling.

"The Boss also told us to learn as much as we could about the U. S. so when we found we had extra time and the girls offered us a trip to tour with them, we jumped at the chance. It was on that trip that we got to know each other so much that we fell in love," said Francois.

Henri added, "We also learned so much about the United States that we concluded the Boss was making a very stupid mistake and kept thinking of ways we could convince him of that."

"However, it never came to that because after he got the mules, he decided he did not need us any longer, paid us off with a bonus, and said, in effect, goodbye. It was perfect timing because we had already decided that we were not going back. We were going to find a way to stay here and become citizens. During the trip, we made notes and collected all the arguments we could to persuade Boss to find a way to become friends with the United States. We recently sent all that information to Boss and hope it will have a good effect," Francois concluded.

"Well, if the girls are happy, I'm happy. I guess traveling can have wonderful results. I met a very smart girl on this trip. She helped me so much in solving a problem I had that I hired her to be my secretary and work with my daughters to recruit students for our new university. Enough of that for now. Let's call the girls and go to dinner."

The girls were still changing when the invitation came producing big sighs of relief. By the time they reached the restaurant, Jacob had arranged for a table for six in a quiet corner.

Jacob put everyone at ease with the question, "Who have you invited to the wedding?"

"Well, who is going to come all the way from France for our wedding?" Ruth replied. "Of course, I sent invitations to all nine of our philanthropists, but I don't expect them to come," Ruth replied.

Much to everyone's surprise and delight, Jacob's philanthropists did come. There were no airlines involved. They all flew over in their private planes. Most of them had been to Las Vegas before and preferred staying at other hotels. The men enjoyed the crap tables while the wives enjoyed the shopping. None went near the slot machines. They all considered themselves too smart for that.

The management of the Las Vegas hotel was delighted to host a full-blown wedding rather than one of those fifteen-minute "I do" quickies. They told Ruth and Eve that they would provide their band and a dance hall plus dinner accommodations. When they asked how many guests were expected, Ruth and Eve replied that they only expected a small group, so when all nine of the philanthropists started showing up with their families, there was quite a lot of scrambling around to accommodate them.

During the dance, after the wedding, Jacob made a point to contact each of the nine philanthropists individually to introduce them to his secretary, Camille, and to ask them to stay over a day so that they could have a meeting to discuss the status of the university program together with his proposal for its future plans. He pointed out that planning was important enough that it must be done now despite the fact that both Ruth and Eve would be off on their honeymoons at the time.

 **CHAPTER FORTY-FIVE**

The University is Renamed

On the day after the wedding, the group met in the conference room of the office that Ruth and Eve had set up. It was a large conference room with a long table in the center provided with fourteen comfortable chairs, six on each side and one at each end. In addition, there were another dozen chairs along the wall.

Jacob and Camille were there early, with Jacob taking one of the end chairs and Camille sitting to his left. As the others came in, they re-arranged the chairs so that they could all sit closely around the table. When they had all arrived, Jacob stood and said, "Thank you for coming. I have been concerned for some time about the question of student enrollment in our University of Religions. I would hate to think that I could become known as the Architect that designed and built a university that was a failure because it could not attract any students."

Jacob was immediately interrupted by several of them nodding in agreement and saying together, "We have been worrying about the same thing," and, "We could have the same problem with finding teachers, so I hope you have something to suggest."

Jacob said, "I do have something to suggest, but I cannot take full credit for it because it is from Camille, and I think it is a brilliant suggestion." He turned to Camille with a proud smile and went on to say, "We should change the name to University of Languages and stress that as the main theme while we offer classes in the various local customs of the people, including their religions. With good salaries, we should easily be able to attract teachers from several countries to come to Las Vegas to teach and, with a little incentive, to bring students with them."

He stopped there for a minute to let it all sink in.

Each person raised their eyebrows, turned back and forth to each of their neighbors, and started to smile and nod their heads. Someone started to clap, followed by the rest. Shouts of, "You're in charge!" "Great idea!" "I was worried for nothing!" "Let's get out of here!" were echoing through the room, and they all left in good spirits, simply waving to Jacob and Camille.

Camille turned to Jacob. "That wasn't as hard as I thought it would be."

"Because they enjoyed your suggestion so much."

"Yes, they did," Camille answered. "And I learned a lot more about the university. Apparently, you are responsible for everything. They don't expect you just to design and build it. They expect you to hire the professors and recruit the students. Can you imagine that? This job you hired me for could last quite a while."

"The longer, the better, as far as I am concerned," he replied.

 # CHAPTER FORTY-SIX

An Almost Meeting

Flying into Tusayan, Hugh and his family, Susan and the three children, Andrew, Barbara, and Charlie, almost filled the small plane. When they de-planed, the local FBI agent met them with his big SUV providing plenty of room for the family and their luggage. He drove them to a nice hotel that Tom had recommended, The Grand Hotel.

They went into the lobby, and as Hugh was registering, he called Susan over and said, "Look at this!" He pushed the register over where she could see it. There above where he was writing were two registrations: Mr. and Mrs. Francois Allard and Mr. and Mrs. Henri Blanchet.

Susan's mouth dropped open, "Can you believe that? What a coincidence!"

Hugh looked over at the FBI agent, who was watching him with just barely a smile on his face.

"Let's get our bags in our rooms and go directly to the Grand Canyon," Hugh said hurriedly.

After settling in, they returned to the SUV and, with the FBI agent driving, proceeded directly to where the mules are usually kept. John Smith was there and came over to the car, pleasantly surprised to see Susan again. He informed them that some of the mules were out being ridden down into the canyon and that those two men, accompanied by their wives, were the same men who tried to buy mules before.

All three children piled out of the car to go and see the few mules that were left, while the adults decided to just wait in the car. John Smith joined the children to make sure both children and mules were safe from each other.

It wasn't long before the four mules were ridden by Francois, Ruth, Henri and Eve arrived. The FBI agent pointed out who was who as they sat unnoticed in the car. Hugh remarked that he hoped Francois and Henri continued through life as innocent as they looked at this moment.

"Don't worry," Susan replied. "The FBI will continue to monitor them to make sure they are not part of a "sleeper cell" planted here."

The children had to be dragged away from John Smith. They were so intrigued by the stories he was telling them. That was his technique to keep them from bothering his mules.

On the way back to the hotel, the children were re-telling those stories and laughing about them.

"Mister Smith told the wildest tales, Mom and Dad. He claimed two of his mules had flown across the Atlantic Ocean!" Charlie said. "I told him that I knew Santa Claus' reindeer could fly, but I never heard of a mule flying."

"He also claimed that the President of the United States was flying by in Air Force One and landed in Las Vegas just to visit with him while he was there! Can you imagine that?" added Andrew.

Hugh remarked, "The telling of good stories has always been a wonderful talent. I wish I knew how to do that."

Other Books by Seth Moorhead

Non-fiction

Your First Golf Lesson
The Secret to Winning Gin
Uncommon Sense
Your Second Golf Lesson

About the Author

Seth Moorhead holds a Bachelor's degree in Aeronautical Engineering and a Master's degree in Business Administration. He is retired from Lockheed Martin and resides in Orlando, Florida.

He was born in Charleston, S. C., and attended The Citadel, U. S. Naval Academy, and Rensselaer Polytechnic Institute. After graduation, he worked at several jobs, including teaching high school mathematics. He worked for Douglas Aircraft in Santa Monica, California, the Naval Air Development Center in Johnsville, Pennsylvania, the Engineering and Research Corporation in Hyattsville, Maryland, and The Martin Company in Orlando, Florida, during which time he attended graduate school at Rollins College and received an MBA degree.

He retired from Lockheed-Martin after 32 years in Advanced Design and Marketing.

More about the Author and the number 4

Mathematicians and others fascinated by numbers may be interested in the pervasiveness of the number 4 throughout the author's life.

He grew up at 64 Montague Street in Charleston, South Carolina, in the same home his mother grew up in. It is a large 4-story home containing 14 fireplaces. It was during a time prior to dial telephones when an operator transferred calls to it at 4499W. He entered high school at the age of 14 and graduated in 1944.

He attended 4 colleges. While working, he applied for and was granted 4 patents. After retiring, he played enough golf at Rio Pinar Country Club to score a hole-in-one on each of the 4 par-3 holes there.

Prior to this book, his first fiction novel, he wrote and published 4 non-fiction books.